Surviving Adverse Seasons

ILLINOIS SHORT FICTION

Surviving Adverse Seasons

Stories by Barry Targan

UNIVERSITY OF ILLINOIS PRESS

Urbana   Chicago   London

"Kingdoms," *Sewanee Review*. vol. 86, no. 3, Summer, 1978

"The Garden," *Salmagundi*, no. 46, Fall, 1979

"The Rags of Time," *Southwest Review*. vol. 64, no. 3, Summer, 1979

"Surviving Adverse Seasons," *Salmagundi*. nos. 31-32, Fall, 1975–
Winter, 1976; reprinted in *Best American Short Stories* (1976).

Library of Congress Cataloging in Publication Data

Targan, Barry, 1932—
  Surviving adverse seasons.
  (Illinois short fiction)
  I. Title.
PZ4.T184Su   [PS3570.A59]   813'.5'4   79-20191
ISBN 0-252-00786-7
ISBN 0-252-00787-5 pbk.

To Ronnie

Contents

Kingdoms

I

My father is somewhere in America, parked in his pick-up at a campsite if he is south, where it is still warm enough to sleep outside under blankets. Or else, if he is north, he is in a cheap hotel in, say, Duluth, in one of those just-off-of-center-city hotels for those who need them. And my father would know them all.

My father is somewhere in America, if nothing has happened to him, as at any moment it might. The last I heard from him was from Topeka. That was four months ago. He called, collect. "Nothing has changed," he said. Whatever else he said—about his health, the condition of the pick-up, the price of clear pine or of copper tubing in Topeka, the weather—what he really called to say was that "Nothing has changed." Not that he expected it to. Not that I did.

When I was ten my mother died in an automobile accident, in a car tumbled across a highway by a blown tire. The Vermont State Police reconstructed the accident for us. For my father, rather. He told me about it later. For twenty-five years I have, from time to time, come crashing out of sleep shouting to her to jump, to live. But she did not.

In 1950, when my mother died, my father was professor of English at Amherst College. He was forty-two and had written three books—about Shakespeare, about Ben Jonson, and about a late seventeenth-century poet of whom nearly no one had heard at that time, Thomas Traherne. My father is supposed to have made him, Traherne, well known. He had also written countless articles about the literature of the sixteenth and seventeenth centuries. Everything he wrote someone would print. And he ranged more widely, too, and could discourse extempore on the latest fiction and poetry or on anything else—boats, painting, butterflies. He had a mighty sweep. He told me all this, *taught* it to me, in all the strange and gorgeous years we shared. After.

In 1951, a year after my mother's death, Milton Carswell, a man only two years younger than my father, married with two children, and a specially good friend of my father's, was rejected for tenure after six years at Amherst.

For other men it might have gone on differently—gone on, at least, at another school or even as an insurance salesman, even as a waiter. But Milton Carswell, by forty, had been broken to the belief that his only true goal in life was to get a job and then to keep it for life. He did not know that about himself until it was too late. He should have worked for civil service, but he became a teacher of Shelley's poetry and Keats's instead. At forty, Milton Carswell, after too many schools, had been judged by the caprice of his profession too long, had been evaluated one time too many, had been weighed in the ever-fining scales beyond his capacity for extension. There was nothing left of him. He had been ground too small, and when the worst wind that his shriveled life had taught him to think he could dream of actually did come, he blew away.

After all the orderly appeals (led by my father) to the various committees were over, after the student demonstrations and the offers of good letters of recommendation from those who had fired him, and after the party at which everybody got drunk and happy like stoic Romans bred out of risible Greeks, after all that, Milton Carswell put his affairs in order and killed himself. No one knew he even had a gun. So few in college have. Perhaps Milton Carswell, wiser by experience in his profession's ways, attuned to them, had prepared.

That was in February. Soon after, my father requested and got a leave of absence for the following year. In late May he bought a pick-up truck and began building it into a movable aluminum house. In those days there were no luxurious, fully equipped pods that you could buy in one hour and back up under and then in one hour drive off, ready to plug in anywhere. And in those days there were no places to plug into. If you traveled the land, then you traveled it on its terms.

My father could use his hands. He worked seven days a week on his truck, building it, modifying it. Long days. At night he charted courses like a navigator on maps. In the middle of June, a dragging week more of my school to go, my father told me his plan. The day after school was over for me, we were going to drive west, across America. Take all summer to do it. The Grand Canyon, Mount Rushmore, Death Valley—I had only to name it.

At eleven I was ready for such a grand adventure, but I was not yet ready to give up my chance as starting pitcher for my Little League team.

I wasn't sure, I told him, that I wanted to go. I mean I told him that I wanted to go but that I wanted to pitch, too. And what about the Y camp in August? For the only time in my life, then or after, he told me I must do what he had decided. So it was settled. On June 23 we drove west on Route 9 out of town, our first destination Chicago, our first stop that day wherever the night caught us.

We never went back.

I mean we never went back to Amherst, to 312 Chelsea Street to a place called home. We went back physically five years later, but as visitors, caravaneers passing through as we had passed through so many other places. I was sixteen and little had changed except me. When the decision had come to sell the house, to cut out completely, I think we were in Salt Lake City, about forty miles south of it on the farthest fringe of the lake. My father had arranged the sale of the house, the sale of much that was in it, the packing and sending to a sister in Harrisburg, Pennsylvania, of what was left, all by telephone and a few letters.

Driving slowly down Chelsea Street that summer day, we stopped nowhere, spoke to no one. And how could I have begun to tell them what had happened?

"Sooner or later," he would tell me, by firelight (where it was good to hear him, whatever he said), or over the hot plate that he lugged about to cook our supper on in the crummy hotel rooms (which I hated), "Sooner or later," he would shout at me, me sitting on the side of the large high single bed we would sleep in together, my feet dangling two inches above the floor, "Sooner or later," he would wave his wooden cooking spoon about, would stir the beans, slice the hard, dark breads he could always find in whatever city we came to, butter it thick for me, hand me a carrot, boil a knockwurst, pour out a jelly glass of milk, "Sooner or later all our corpuscles are bursting and rotting one by one. Our neurons atrophy second by second. Tick-tock, kid. Tick-tock, my little warrior." Then he would turn from me and weep. My own sorrow for him then was infinite, though I could not name it or comprehend it.

At the end of supper, after the few dishes (washed in the hallway bathroom), we would play chess. Or listen to the radio, listening, between each country and western song, to the distant pounding voices from Del Rio, Texas, or Wheeling, West Virginia, selling illustrated Rembrandt Bibles bound in white gold-embossed calfskin or two-foot-high carved imitation onyx crucifixes with simulated ivory Jesuses hanging upon them. TV was only beginning and was not ordinary, and where we stayed it would never be available except in the lobby of stuffed armchairs and spring-sprung sofas with dazed old men fraying apart in them.

Or else, and frequently, he would read to me. Sometimes he would read to me a book my equal: *Call of the Wild* or *Greatest Baseball Players of the Century*. But mostly, too impatient for the deceptions of children's literature, anxious for the great deceptions, he would read to me from his own vaster store. He would read, complete with commentary, say, from *Hamlet:*

> And let me speak to the yet unknowing world
> How these things came about: so shall you hear
> Of carnal, bloody, and unnatural acts,
> Of accidental judgements, casual slaughters,

> Of deaths put on by cunning and forced cause,
> And, in this upshot, purposes mistook
> Fall'n on the inventors' heads: all this can I
> Truly deliver.

"How about that, my young friend? How about that?"
What he meant was that nothing was bitter enough. Nothing
that he had taught back in Amherst, nothing that the greatest
artists wrote, none of it prepared us for the terribleness of our
dispossessed lives, our unaccommodated lives.
"Literature is too redemptive," he would shout, hunched over
the wheel of the truck in the earlier, increasingly manic years.
Suffering was his theme.

By the end of the first summer, too close to the end of it for
me reasonably to get back east in time for school, we had circled
out of Seattle, climbed the switchbacked roads and then trails up
the Cascades and rolled down the eastern slope of them into the
slowly drying basin of what becomes central Washington. We
stopped for a week in Walla Walla. That was where my father
did his first skilled labor, tested, I think, the possibility of the
life he came at last to lead.
We had stopped for our lunch on some boundary of Walla
Walla where the city feathered into countryside. In the morning,
before we set out, he would make sandwiches and often a thermos
of soup so when we stopped at noon, or whenever, we were ready.
But it was not time he was trying to save; later I saw that it was
time he was trying to spend.
That day we were eating lunch in a small park, the remnant
of a larger woods that had been trimmed down and left to be
surrounded by the dozens of houses and hundreds of people
coming quickly. All through our lunch my father was uncharac-
teristically silent. We had been following baseball through the
summer and guessing at it as the pennant races drew down to
October and the series. I had carried across the continent all my
baseball cards and had added to them at every opportunity through

the land. We talked baseball a lot. The same things. He would tell me the same stories of his young baseball adventures, and I would give him statistics. I would quote extensively the facts of baseball printed on the backs of cards in type too small for any but the youngest eyes to see or care about.

But that day in Walla Walla we sat in the tiny park and did not talk. We ate silently as he looked across at the men who were building the houses, who had also stopped working to eat. When we had finished and they had finished, he got up and walked over into the clutter of the project, the skeletons of studs and rafters and joists and headers that looked more handsome in their honesty than would the gimcrackery that would be hoisted upon them. I had been with him when he had done that before, had walked with him as he observed and muttered at the shabbiness, at the fraud of the buildings. They would not last a generation, he told me, but I did not know how long a generation was.

Today was different. He found the man who seemed to be managing the site and asked him for a job. And he got it. The houses had to be finished before the winter, before the snow, which, in that high plateau of the country, came early.

He began work the next morning, crawling across sheets of plyscore, hammering them onto the rafters for the roof. On that first day I waited down below. After each roof he and the crew he worked in would move down the row to the next house. I would follow, watch them climb up the ladder, listen to the hammer bursts of nailing, and wait. I could not think what else to do. It was the first time I had been alone. He had not talked much that night about his taking the job. He may not have known himself what to say.

But on the second day I sought my own necessities. I was eleven, getting on toward twelve and a good size for my age. And I had had a summer on the road by now. New places did not stop me as they had earlier. All my places by now were new.

That second day, Wednesday, I walked down the rise from the housing project farther into the city, keeping to Lincoln Avenue like a thread raveling out behind me so that I would know my way back. In fifteen long blocks I came to a schoolyard where boys were playing, throwing a basketball up against the wall to where a hoop should be, but there was none. They passed off, drove hard for the basket, hooked or leaped up for arching one-handers and scored or did not score by measurements or agreements of their own. I did not know why they were not in school. And I do not remember wondering then. Perhaps I simply assumed that they were like me, of that band afloat now in a sea of different circumstance, no longer moored—or tethered—to places like home or school. Or games like others played.

They were all older than I, around fifteen I'd guess, maybe more. They played hard, and sometimes a team would win and a new game would start. I watched carefully for nearly an hour, coming closer, until I was noticed.

"You want to play?" the tallest boy asked me. "You want to play?"

"I don't know how," I said.

"You don't know how to play basketball?"

"I don't know how to play without the hoop."

"It's easy," he said. "Here." He pushed the ball at me very hard and it bounced painfully off my fingers. I picked the ball up.

"Shoot," he commanded. I lofted the ball as best I could to where the basket should have been. "Terrific," he shouted. "Great shot. You're on my team." So we began. But with or without a true hoop, I could not play with them. They were too large and fast for me, but more: they were playing a different game, different even from the imaginary game I had watched. For I was the game. The center of the circle. "It," the flag to capture, the creature to be run.

The ball bounced off my head. I turned. I was hit with the ball from the other side. I turned there and was hit again from behind.

"Come on, man," my captain shouted. "Get with it. Hang onto the ball, man. How we going to make a play without the ball?" And I would be hit. They ringed me with laughter. I did not try to move through them, though no one offered to bar me.

I stood the thudding of the ball as an animal in shock will wait for the net of ravening hunters to close in upon it, and not outrun them as it might. How could I end what I could not comprehend? Until I turned once in time to see the ball come. I caught it and threw it hard like a baseball into his face, smashing his nose. After his scream, after his blood, they moved at me with their fists, kicking, punching.

And then they were gone, like a squall that can come on a perfect day and break down trees and strip the blossoms in a garden, batter wheat with hail and go as quickly, leaving the day as perfect, perhaps even clearer, brighter, as still. I was in the schoolyard, not too damaged, alone. I walked out onto Lincoln Avenue and began the long, slow, easy climb up out of the city to its edge.

What had touched me? How could I imagine what had happened, me, this child of perfect peace? I would ask my father. He who knew everything, would know. He would tell me. But when I got back to the construction site I found him waiting for me by our truck, beaten too.

His lip was split and blood was crusted on it. His left eye was red and puffy. The top two buttons of his work shirt were popped off, the collar slightly ripped. When I saw him, only then did I cry. But when he saw me, bruised and cracked myself, and understood as I told him, sobbing, about my own wounds, he laughed, rose up and whooped to heaven.

"Omens, little friend," he said to me, his arm across my shoulder. "Portents. Auguries." He got water from the truck and washed my face, opened a beer from our cooler and poured me some and drank the rest. Then we set off, slowly, down my Lincoln Avenue, past the now-empty schoolyard, into the center of Walla Walla and across it and toward the south.

"What's in Oregon?" he asked at a crossroad. "Pick something." I had the map.

"Pendleton. It's about sixty miles. It's right on a main road."

So that is where we went, to a small aspen grove of a state campsite just above the city where through the October night, all night, great machines roared westward and north across the sky protecting us.

By our small fire he told me that he had slipped on the roof and had dropped his hammer on a man, on the man's shoulder, and the man came up onto the roof to fight him. The man would accept no apology, no explanation. Even after the brief fight, the man would have no containment, no calm, as if the accident, so close to being worse, to maybe killing him, had stained him, violated him irreparably. He was angry like a madman. But he was not mad. The foreman settled him by sending him off the job for the rest of the day. He fired my father. It was a solution.

And as my father told me this, expanding what he told, elaborating, recalling, noting and annotating the way a scholar might upon a myth, he would nod briefly, fiercely. To his own incident and perception he added my bizarre attack, mixing and mumbling incantations like an alchemist amidst his limbecks and retorts, approaching distillation. Then, like the embers in our little fire, he glowed and brightened and at last burst into renewed flame, a harrowing wind blowing through him forever.

"Now might I do it pat," he cracked across the night so that I stood up at that stabbing sound. "And now I'll do it." He raised his arms to the stars. "Be thou my good," he said, not to the stars he gestured at, but to vaster intelligences. I was frightened. And not frightened. Thrilled, rather. Enamoured. He was marvelous, if baffling, but attuned to regions beyond me, I was sure. I had faith. "Go pee," he said to me.

He helped me into my bunk in the truck and told me my nighttime story. Not that it was always a tale; sometimes it was history or theories of bird migration and such, or poems. Sometimes he sang. But from the beginning of time, my time, he had always been there to tell me something. Tonight he told me of someone called Actaeon, a great hunter, who chanced to look upon the goddess Artemis while she was bathing—alas, a sin. In punishment she turned Actaeon into a stag so that his own hounds turned on him, pursued, and killed him.

"It isn't fair," I said as I sank down. "It wasn't his fault."

"Precisely," my father said. "Yes. Exactly." He gripped my hand tight, hard with his excitement about his own understanding and what he thought was mine. "But remember this." His whisper was like a knife. "The gods are not just. But they are *right*." But even if I had understood, I was too tired to care; so even if he was telling me one of life's enormous and valuable secrets, I would have to learn it again in other ways, in a different time, not now. Then he leaned over me and kissed my forehead as always. Always.

In the morning he explained that I was to stay by myself for this day and night and part of the next day. We set up a tent, arranged what needed arranging, and he drove off. He told me I would be all right. Just stay put. And don't worry.

I read and walked about the aspen grove, sat by a small stream watching late striders on the autumn-low water of the pond, made my supper and went into the tent early. He returned the following morning by eleven o'clock.

"Let's go. Move it." In twenty minutes we were packed up and gone. To Boise eastward, I think, or maybe farther.

After ten miles he told me what he had done. "I joined up," he said. "We enlisted in the war. I went back to Walla Walla and broke his truck. Ah, the daring of it! When they were on the last house I opened his hood and worked an acid paste into his distributor, some on the coil, here and there in other spots. In a day, maybe two, his truck will need a lot of fixing. I did it. Me." He looked sideways at me as the land rose and fell and rose all about us, stiffening into Idaho and the Rockies. "Do you know what I did?" he asked.

"Sure. You told me just now. The truck."

"No. Not that. More. Deeper. More important. Listen! Listen! I did a small and petty thing. A vicious thing. Me. And I am *pleased* by that. *An irrevocable act of violence on my own.* Now let's see what it's like, huh? Right? From now on?"

"What what's like?" I asked. But he did not answer that, or even hear it, I think. He hunched up over the steering wheel and squinted out, smiling. If he could have answered what I asked, we might have driven other roads. Or nowhere. But he could not answer me. That is what we were to seek. That is why.

II

For three years we traveled in a great swooping peregrination of this country—Lincoln, Wichita, Little Rock—like a soaring bird in the buffeting wind of his necessity. We rose on the thermals of his excitement, we fell through low valleys—Minneapolis, Lexington, Charleston, or Flagstaff or Carson City. We traveled north or east as the gusts sweeping through him took us, settling from time to time to work or to observe or for my father to recapitulate, to gather up his evidences and refine his briefs against life and its chronicles in these, the assizes of our existence, where the judges were his own Furies. And yet not fury, not anger; more a furiousness, the passionateness of accomplishment, really, and not frustration; for what had compelled him out of Amherst and the sinecure of his living still sustained him now. Each day he found a renewing marvel in being right, in being free now to be right.

In those years he was like a wire singing and hot with the energy of countless messages crowding and blazing through it. For him, his verifications were everywhere: the poets had failed—the first hard cutting wave of mind upon oblivion, the last phalanx of civilized defense. All for naught.

"But not us, kiddo. None of the monkdom of literature for us, right? No easy outs. Here is where we are now living, right smack in the world's wind, taking this chill from it right into the bones to give the lie in the teeth to consciousness, which doth make cowards of us all. Yes," he would emphasize, smacking his spoon upon a log or table top, his tin cup of wine upon a rock. "Listen to this." Then he would recite to me or read to me from books— stories, poems, plays, poking at the texts with his finger and poking through their misinforming fabric. Perhaps he read or recollected too selectively, allowing his fierce argument to follow a convenient vein; but on balance I think not. From singing Homer to the strident present, pessimism, despair, the bitterness of the primary truth of the human condition—it was all diluted, attenuated either in religious faiths or ideologies and their assumptions of order and equity, or in the "Blakean humpty-dump of the personal vision," as he styled it. But at the critical point, in the fell crunch of circumstance, writer after writer backed off, accepted some validating moral structure in the universe, insisted upon or suggested *some* reason for it all, this progress of a mortal soul upon this thoroughfare of woe.

"This thoroughfare of woe," he bellowed. "Chaucer," he told me. "That comes close. Chaucer nearly makes it sometimes." He told me about Alison sticking her brazen ass out into the night and immortality. "The *comic* sense. That's maybe all you can trust. There are others," he would nod wisely, knowingly. "Moments, lines, stanzas, chapters, something here and there. But nothing altogether. No. At the edge of truth's abyss, they all step back, even Willie S. But not us, huh, bub? Now that we know?" Then he would reach over and put his hand on me somewhere—my knee, my arm, my head—and leave it there, forgetting it, content only then.

And so he would lecture on. Reading, declaiming, interpreting, haranguing, wrenching apart the heartstrung words of man, stridently arguing me to his side, determined that I, at least, should make no mistake about it, and certainly not repeat his. But if he told me the stories about which he fumed and railed, so too did we create tales of our own. And gather others.

We evolved a method of existing. For about a year at first we would drive around in whatever community we found ourselves until he located a construction site—a single house going up, or a shopping center, or even more often somebody repairing storm windows or the steps to his front porch. Or working on his car. My father would inquire, offer, bargain, and surprisingly he would get the work, at least enough, replacing someone who had not shown up on the job, or by knowing what to do just when the homeowner or car repairer did not. And he worked cheaply—an enticement to a crew chief, who could keep the difference between my father's wages and what was recorded. Unions posed an obstacle, especially in large constructions, but even then there were ways around them. There were always ways around, and other ways. I think that is what my father wanted to know and to prove. Certainly. Perfectly. The non-Euclidean necessity to human action, the negativity of moral space.

Later on he refined his methods. We would walk about until he found a problem—a broken gate, dangling gutters, a pane of glass that was cracked or needed reglazing. He would ring the bell and make his offer, a clean, well-mannered man and his apprentice. We were seldom refused the work. And after, once he had done his first job, then chairs with loose rungs were found, dripping faucets, doors that stuck. And he would fix them, learning much as he went along, but learning quickly.

Frequently we were fed. And interrogated. He would invent, sometimes so wildly that I would go out to the truck with my wonder, embarrassment, and laughter at who he had turned us into—the two of us displaced in a hundred ways by fate in a thousand guises: the loss of the farm, the depletion of our marginal gold mine, the burning down of the small hardware business, the crash of our independent cargo delivery airplane, even the sinking of our fishing boat. From all our disasters we were striking out anew, crossing to a new coast for a new start.

More and more I came to wait for the history he would create for us, excited to know who we were now, this time, what we had passed through, where we had been, where we were going. Some of those fragments that he quickly hewed out of thin air I wished I had been; they seemed then so substantial to me, sharply faceted with details of purpose, carved with a point and direction to their movement.

And his auditors were unfailingly distressed, but heartened, too. We were brave events for them, and they seldom asked more than he told—as if the privilege of intimacy had already been too great, and was a gift not to be abused, but to be somehow reciprocated. Often I was given good clothing, shoes, books, games—so much that my father would sell it at thrift shops along our twisting course.

Outside in our truck, driving off, he would present me his latest evidence. "Fiction," he would shout. "See what it does?"

So we beat on, sometimes driving a thousand hard miles in two days, sometimes roaming softly through a small district for a week or even more. Mostly we avoided the larger cities, where it was expensive to live on the edge of things. And less pleasant and more dangerous. But he insisted that nothing be totally avoided, and that for us to take a different road for a good reason was as fruitless as it had been for Oedipus to flee Corinth to his doom. Thus I came to Sophocles. I remember objecting to the riddle of the Sphinx. I thought it was a dumb riddle. "It could of been something else. I mean the answer didn't *have* to be Man." At that he quickly swerved to the roadside, stopped the truck, and clasped my head into his arms. "Oh right, oh, yes," he said. I could hardly breathe. "Oh what a sweetheart. Oh what a head have I got here." And he squeezed me until I gasped and cried out. And giggled, cross and amazed at the same time. He was irresistible.

As in St. Louis. In August, along the low, river-level bank of St. Louis, we drove slowly up an industrial street called Fillion Place, looking for a used auto parts store he had located in the yellow pages. He needed a throw-out bearing for our clutch, which was beginning to slip badly. Fillion Place was grimy and black, buildings and windows so deeply stained and crusted by carbon exhaust and oil that even on the sunniest days the light was absorbed out of the air, leaving a husk of gloom. Delivery trucks were all around, in the street and on the thin sidewalk. Steel drums of substances and crates were piled up, intermixed with refuse and strewn packaging. In the air was a seamless sound of gears and motors and tailgates banging and voices ordering things about.

Near where the auto parts store should have been, a small explosion blew out a second-floor window, white steam sprayed out in a rolling billow and died to a small hiss, even as the last glass pattered and tinkled to the ground and onto our truck. A man in a clean summery business suit ran out of the building, looked up and down Fillion Place, which had noticed nothing, and then up at the window. Then he saw us.

"What do you want? What are you looking at? Go on, get out of here." He turned back to the shattered window and the thin stream. "Jesus," he said.

"You want it fixed or not?" my father said.

"What?" the man said, turning again. "You some kind of wise guy? Go on, get out of here."

"I fix things. I can fix that."

"Listen," the man said. "One more time. Get out of here."

But my father got out of the truck. The man jumped back, frightened. He started to raise his hands as if my father had threatened to hit him. "Whaa," he croaked.

"I've got to buy a part," my father said, and pointed to the store two buildings down. Trucks shook by. He walked away. I watched the man. He leaned back against the building, looking down at his shoes. The steam was falling against the building, condensing in a long wet black sharply pointed tongue descending the wall. If he did not move soon, the black slick would pierce him. At the last instant he came over to the truck.

"Is that your father?"

"Yes."

"What's he do?"

"He fixes things."

"What's that mean?"

"We drive around fixing things, working." I pointed into the back of our truck, at the heavy arrangement of tools and materials.

"That's all you do? Anywhere?"

"That's all." I explained a little more. The man walked back to the wall and began to pace. When my father came out of the store, the man approached him. They talked and concluded. I had seen it many times before.

We unloaded the tools my father selected and locked up the truck and started for the building.

"Leave the boy," the man said, but my father would not.

The second floor we mounted to was a distillery, a perfect small bootleg operation, as my father would later explain.

The rest is mostly small confusions that jigsaw together in my memory. I remember the man hovering about my father and arguing with him about everything, at every move—turning off the steam, opening certain valves, making other adjustments.

Still, the work went on. I wandered about between hundred-pound sacks of sugar piled twenty high, drums of malt extract stenciled in New Jersey, wooden boxes of aluminum-foil-wrapped blocks of dried yeast. At the very rear of the warehouse some kind of grain, maybe wheat, stood in a mountain with its peak touching the trap door it must have been dumped from. Rats scurried in and around the grain. I ran back to the apparatus of tubing and closed vessels and boilers.

My father was working in and around the whole thing. The man had removed his coat; his shirt was soaked and sticking completely to his skin, making him ghostly pink and glowing. He was urging him to hurry, but as my father worked, he talked. He asked questions about the distillery, made comments about how to improve the operation, expressed his admiration for it all. The man grew angry at the talk. My father provoked him.

"You're crazy," he said to my father, "talking so much. You should hurry up and get out of here. You're in trouble just being here now, let me tell you. You know that? You can figure that out, can't you?"

But my father persisted, wondering what label, if any, they used, and how they handled distribution.

Then the other men came. They argued among themselves. My father told me softly to get over to the stairs. Then the tangle of pipes and vats and spigots blew apart, or, more accurately, cracked open at a dozen turns and points. Steam, alcohol fumes, ambrosial yeastiness puffed through the warehouse and out into Fillion Place. I scrambled down the stairs, my father thudding behind me. Into the truck, careening down Fillion Place, up into St. Louis, through it, past it, beyond it, my father was whooping, slapping on the steering wheel.

"We're on the lam," he shouted. "The gang is after us."

I looked behind. He might have been right. I did not see why he should not have been right.

"Fugitives," he hollered, delighted. "Outlaws. Marked by the Mafia. Beyond the Pale. Wanted men. Godalmighty," he yipped in his pleasure and wonderment. "Talk about luck." He tooted the horn. We did not stop until Columbia. And then not again until Odessa, on our way to Kansas City.

III

Who was my father now from whom he had been? I remember that when my mother was alive my father was a quiet man, but not subdued or scholarly in that sense, or pale and soft and silent. He had always been active, busy, a good companion for talking or fishing, and sometimes exuberant. But he was reflective, quiet that way, as if he was always looking at and through what he was saying, or hearing, considering and adjusting his thoughts within an elegant context, a splendid fretwork of infinite but controlled complexity. And I remember him from Amherst days as being orderly and neat in his affairs, efficient and economical, yet without being overbearing and pinched about it: precise, I suppose, in the way of strong and confident men. There was a constant *tone* about him, and I battened in the safety and constancy. My mother's energy and urgency lit my life against and through the firm foil and lens of my father. There were no dark corners then.

He was, I think now, in those early days on Chelsea Street, a man who had made up his mind early, who had come to all his conclusions once and for all. He was a man who had used his good and well-furnished mind, his bright humor and excellent health, to examine the principle of things, the *grain* of ideas, the *weft* of thought, and thus could live abundantly in that illumination. And calmly, open minded but certain. Sure.

So it was not, either simply or complexly, the deaths of my mother and Milton Carswell, precipitants though they were, that caused or sustained this new extension. For in an important way I do not think he changed. I think he continued to examine as ever the principle of things, the grain and weft, but came, because of his strengths of spirit and qualities of mind, to a new perception of the universe so staggeringly different from his early conclusions and desires that the joy of his wonder and the consequence of his rage could not help but follow, as if a man of his attainments had no other choice. Given a place to stand, a fulcrum and a lever long enough, Archimedes claimed that he could move the earth. Now my father believed that he had found such a place, such a fulcrum, and day by day he thought to prove again that proposition, explore its ramifications, develop corollaries, and nudge the planet inch by inch into another orbit.

But there is more to any explanation of my father's behavior: there was the expiation he demanded for his special guilt of having ever accepted the artificial mysteries of the arranged—*nice*—ambiguities of literature and the hope engendered. So he also set out to atone for that faith, to fathom mystery truly now by becoming a part of mystery. To offer no elegiac stanzas for Milton Carswell, no tragic threnody for his wife. No. To offer instead a brilliant definition of the human predicament, and in no other way but to thrust himself into it, like a scientist like Haldane, who injected himself first with his serums because he who could understand the results must be the first to venture.

Who was my father now from whom he had been on Chelsea Street in Amherst, on autumn afternoons when his students and their parents walked through the dry, scuttering leaves toward their pleasant, sedate suppers in Little Lord Jeff, dining upon their expectations for their sons, inebriant with dreams?

He was a man intent beyond our imagining to break off from the safety of the past, of heritage and tradition as it had made him, and then to build something else, creating a new ethic as he went along through life now for the first time. In our travels whenever he would stop long enough for us to settle for a moment, as he would talk to a customer or a man in a lumberyard or to anyone at all—for he could not do other than talk now—endlessly, he would slip into the twang or drawl or nasality of the region, adapt in his own speech the local patois. Wherever we were he would assume the shape of his condition—the squint of a sailor's sun-blazed eyes, the slight stoop and lean of mountain men, the bowed waddle of the rancher, the narrow hunch of city people. He resisted nothing. And that was his giddy pleasure now—to bend to every wind, be etched by circumstance like water running sharply in a canyon, and to come again and again to the same conclusion, that we were all beyond the perceived arrangements of philosophy or science and, above all, the language of the poets. It was a truth he read in everything.

But there was contradiction enough so that, triumphant and braying about the failure of old visions as he was now, I still sensed in him the other man I had known, and for a time I even expected him, that vestigial self, to come forth at last, to step out of this new man prancing about upon this stage he had turned our lives into, and to take us both back to where we had started. But he never did.

Still, it was as if he had not altogether rid himself of his old burden as he supposed he had, but had instead undergone a terrific compression in which all the atoms of ancient compassion had coalesced into a core too small to see but of enormous density, a core of old faiths hot and molten but trapped.

At least that is how I interpret the incidents in which poetry occasionally seemed to matter to him again in the old way, as in Montana once, near the town of Riley, at that perfect gradient where the prairie slips off from the Rockies and fits down as neatly as a plowed field about the Missouri River as it slowly turns southward. We had made camp for the night, were braced against the cold of prairie nights, and now was the good time for me, the best time, the two of us, fed and nearly drowsing, between jobs, nothing but now.

In the dark the river flung itself by us not far away. Morning and afternoon we had fished in it, but mainly in the rich, glossy tributaries where the speckled trout leaped endlessly. The fire sank. He put his hand upon my head and then suddenly sang out like a benediction across the grasses hissing in the wind and against the mountains.

When I have seen by Time's fell hand defaced
The rich proud cost of outworn buried age;
When sometime lofty towers I see down-razed
And brass eternal slave to mortal rage;
When I have seen the hungry ocean gain
Advantage on the kingdom of the shore,
And the firm soil win of the watery main,
Increasing store with loss and loss with store;
When I have seen such interchange of state,
Or state itself confounded to decay;
Ruin hath taught me thus to ruminate,
That Time will come and take my love away.

He stood up quickly and shouted now again,

That Time will come and take my love away.

And again, quietly, a mutter.

That Time will come and take my love away.
This thought is as a death, which cannot choose
But weep to have that which it fears to lose.

Oh, those were the marvelous times when we touched each other
across my mother's death, for in no other way could we speak of
it, in all those years down all those roads. But in the nights like
Montana I knew him best, and understood best, in my child's
way, the cost of his strange renunciation, the price of his disdain
for all our past.

My mother's death did not cause in me pain in the ordinary
sense; rather, the pain of loss, of absence, a missing. I did not
miss *her*; I missed what my life had felt like when she had been
there to ravel me up in her sweep and gaiety. But it was into that
emptiness that he rushed. Wherever I turned he was there, filling
me up. My days were full of jewels flung about me like largess,
gifts ceaselessly bestowed by this Prince who knew nothing any
longer of boundaries. No more. I went his way with him into
freedom and healed, bathed in the torrent that he had become

until I grew strong in it myself and swam along with him, free as he would have me, as he wanted me to be. Only at those times when the poetry came over him did I remember that there had even been another way than this. And why we were here.

And in the Mojave, where the desert stars glinted and spangled like ice-coated trees in morning sun, I listened to the grains of sand knocked loose by the hunting spiders crashing about like boulders. All around I listened to the open death of creatures, quick and graceful, the sidewinder stalking the waiting mouse, the owl dropping down on the snake, green-eyed coyotes ranging wide of us. Then I heard him, softly now, in the old voice from long ago, to himself, to the night, to the immensity of the desert in that night, as if in the center of galaxies,

> Meanwhile, the mind from pleasure less,
> Withdraws into its happiness:
> The mind, that ocean where each kind
> Does straight its own resemblance find;
> Yet it creates, transcending these,
> Far other worlds, and other seas;
> Annihilating all that's made
> To a green thought in a green shade.

And down I dove.

IV

But who was I now from whom I had been? For if he had departed in limitless flight, an Icarus contriving through outer darknesses, had I willingly flown too? Or had I been drawn with him, inevitably, like a satellite, a moon lit brilliantly by his urgent but reflected light, secure in his gravity, fixed by his great mass, even if bound?

Not that I thought such things; not then, of course, or not that way. But later, when I came to be taught by others that dreams were metaphors of our interior terrains, I could never accept that idea so easily, for my dreams in those years seemed exactly like my life—intensely detailed, sharp and pungent and spikey with substance—and as fleeting.

Only along a thin line did my dreams and my life run together like the brown, scudding foam of a tide rising or falling in fractions of inches across a beach. There is the sea and there is the sand, but at some instant, at some point, the sea and the sand mix into something different from either; when exactly, or where, can never be told. So at times did my waking life and my dreams bond in a fluttery-edged mantle, and then I would dream clear and precise vistas that I had never seen, though I constructed them out of all my days, or else I passed awake through colossal events without remark or memory.

But on either side of that line I was never disoriented. I never confused which was the dream, or the reality, or the insubstantiality between. I could always tell which was the dream because it was shaped, hard and firm with angles and curves, posts and lintels and arches that met and bore up the feeling, the *condition*, of structure. My dreams were as rigid as my life was not—tight with streets and fences, gardens planted and ripening, a sense of *place* elegant with design, design as pervasive as a perfume. And I could tell my dreams from my waking life because in my dreams my father was never there.

Only once and only for an instant did I stumble, trip upon a dream that had come true.

For three days we had worked at installing irrigation pipes and getting the pumps to pull the water through them smoothly across the flat fields of Amiston, about fifty miles northwest of Houston. Amiston is gone now, become a school district and a zip code of Houston's suburbs, and the fields we worked in—cotton making a last stand in this part of Texas—are all paved. But then we yanked countless lengths of the light aluminum tubing into place and snapped them together with special water-tight fittings. The aluminum would quickly draw the heat of the sun and build it up, so that even through the heavy work gloves the work was hot and uncomfortable. My father had found the job at the gas stop he had made outside of Amiston. A question or two, a sense of the season's necessities, and directions were all he needed.

We showed up at Kurt Doachmann's house at dawn. I did not see the house then; I was still in the camper, hanging onto a little more sleep as best I could, like a sailor tight in his bunk, swinging through a storm. I could tell where I was in the world through the motion of the truck—highways, farms, cities; asphalt, concrete, or dirt. After thirty minutes while my father negotiated, we started off, more roughly than before, into the farm proper, riding the tractor ruts like rails.

For three days we stayed out at the farthest edge of Doachmann's land, working. Besides my father and me, there were two men whom Doachmann would bring out in the morning and pick up at night. Doachmann himself would drive the truck with the irrigation pipes, timing it so that he arrived with a new load just as we clamped down on the last pipe of the last load and before we could stop for a rest. He didn't care if we rested; all he wanted was his work done. He knew how many pipes he needed to string together each day, and that was what he brought us. His years of experience had taught him how to pace his help.

At the end of that third day Doachmann had trouble with some switches in the pumps. He could not fill his pipes, his fields. But my father worked out the problem cleverly, saving Doachmann a long trip for a replacement and the cost of an electric circuit and harness that would have cost dearly. After Doachmann had taken the other two men away, he came back and paid. We were cleaned up by then, sitting by the camper finishing supper in failing light. Doachmann sat down with us and took out a bottle of whiskey which he offered to my father, a drink which he took straight.

Doachmann liked my father's style. No cotton to dry up in a week of hot wind blowing at the wrong time through the young shoots like a devil's breath. No red dust to wash out of your clothing three times a day, to hose off your car, off your house. No watching the perfect, unblemished sun go down night after night, pulling you into a merciless, leathery bankruptcy. And if there was irrigation now, so there were the pumps that failed, the rising cost of the aluminum tubing, the water table dropping lower each year as farmers and towns and Houston sucked harder at the earth. There was the price of cotton falling to its knees beneath the pummeling of the cotton from Ghana, from Mozambique, from every goddamn place on earth where it always rained enough and the dirt was rich and new.

They had a couple of drinks, maybe more, when Doachmann said, "You. Now you go wherever you need to be. That's fine. Oh that's fine." My father did not answer. It was the kind of statement that he could enjoy, play with, make mean everything or nothing. "I know this oil rig off toward Abilene," Doachmann went on. "Maybe three hundred miles. Joseph Luft. One well, one man, all alone running the whole thing. You'd like to know Joseph Luft. He'd like to know you. He'd pay you, too. For what he needs fixed and done." Doachmann laughed. "He needs it all fixed. Everything. He'd pay you good." He took another drink. But he was not getting drunk. If anything, he was clearer. "I'll take you there. I'll go with you. In a week you could do it. Make more in a week than in a month of this." He meant the irrigation pipes. "It's nothing to be missed, I tell you. A rig like that. One man. Jesus." He slapped his leg. "We'll leave the boy with my wife and family down at the house." He stopped to think a minute, as if considering from my father's point of view. "It's a good family," he said. "They'll take fine care of him." Then, "I'm a good man," he said to my father. "There's nothing *funny* about this. It's just . . . a chance," he said.

But my father understood well enough how other men looked up from their patterns at his truck and saw the Norseman's prow, the trapper's snowshoe track, heard voyageurs singing over the boiling of the rapids. "What do you think?" he asked me. It came at me too quickly to think. I had not been apart from him for years, not even for a single night. Only in my dreams.

"Sure," I said before I could think of anything.

In the morning, when he left me at Doachmann's house and took Doachmann for his ride to Joseph Luft's one-man oil rig, I looked about and found my dream ringing hard as fact.

Doachmann's house was long and low in the prairie style, a

When this is over.

Bring it with.

Lionel sat in a broken rocking chair watching the television, which was perched on a shelf between two pink-shaded lamps. Mae closed her ears to it and looked out the front window at the late snow on the sidewalks.

Eighteen, said Lionel.

What, asked Mae, turning.

She's got to pick a number to win.

Four, said Mae, squinting to follow the action on the tiny screen. The audience applauded and bright tinny music filled the air.

By God four was it, said Lionel. You would've been there Mae, you would've won.

What'd she get?

Washer dryer and eight hunnerd dollars.

Ha, said Mae. That's just exactly my luck, ain't it?

Lionel shook his head and Mae stood to walk around the store. Did you ever stop to think that maybe we got stuff worth money we don't even know about?

Like what, said Lionel.

Well how should I know. If I knew about it I'd have the money instead. I mean something a rich collector'd want.

Maybe one of them pictures?

Mae stooped, grunting, to the canvases stacked in a corner. Like this one? she asked, holding up a mountain landscape.

Lionel shrugged. It's pretty.

It don't have to be pretty. It just has to be artistic, said Mae, but she let the painting drop. Maybe one of these cake plates, she said. She knew Lionel wasn't listening any more and she herself wasn't convinced. Three years ago Mae sold a punchbowl set to an antique dealer for seventy dollars, but that had only happened once.

We just don't have any luck, she said aloud. Lionel leaned back in the rocker and another slat came out of the back. That's the only reason anyone else is in better shape than we are, they got luck. You hear me?

Lionel was asleep, his head thrown back. In his thin neck the

Adam's apple stood out, a hard knot of skin with blue veins on either side. Jesus, said Mae. She pushed a pile of saucepans from a shelf; they slammed to the floor and rolled under the furniture. Lionel's eyes flickered open, then closed. The pattern of his breathing did not change. Jesus, said Mae.

A discontent began to grow in her. When she added up the day's sales, just as the figures were rounding into a pleasant sum, Mae would put down her pencil and ask herself what good it was doing. The neat columns of numbers brought her no satisfaction. Lionel told her she was working too hard. So she tried sleeping late in the mornings and not going out in the truck any more than she had to. This only made her restless and started her worrying about the bills.

She tried to talk about her feelings to the people who came into the store. Seems like the harder you work, the less you get done, she'd say. The farmers with chapped faces and faded eyes agreed, thinking of the bad weather, the broken combine, the price of feed. The women, with children hobbling their legs, they agreed. I love my kids but there's times I wished they belonged to somebody else. It was some comfort to talk like this, but after a while there was nothing left to say, and they parted with the same sense of defeat as before.

Spring never happens all at once in Ohio. First there are treacherous warm days, when people go about in shirt sleeves. Then a week of cold rain. Then it stops, and the fields turn from brown to sodden olive green. Crocuses and daffodils come out, but a late snow is liable to leave them withered and broken-headed. Sometimes the good weather holds, but not often.

It was that sort of bright, uncertain day when Mrs. Cherry came in looking for brass bedsteads. She was a large woman with a bosom that jutted like the prow of a ship. Her husband had made money in hardware, so she spoke with a certain stiffness that was supposed to be gracious condescension. She wore Jungle Gardenia perfume, which she ordered six bottles at a time from Cleveland.

I'm not interested in anything damaged, she told Mae. Just a good brass bedstead. Of course I don't want to pay too much either.

Well, said Mae, I don't know. They were standing in one of the back rooms. Iron bedsprings were stacked against the walls, tangled like the hair of crazy women. Mae stubbed out a cigarette on the cement floor and dragged a headboard to the center of the room. This here's brass.

Mrs. Cherry took a step back and frowned. It doesn't look like brass, she said.

Just needs polishing. Scrub it with Barkeep's Friend and it'll shine up. As long as it ain't gone green it's all right.

Well, said Mrs. Cherry, and Mae could tell by her voice that she wasn't going to buy it. They walked to the front of the store and Mrs. Cherry reapplied her lipstick in a cloudy mirror on the wall.

A nice day, said Mae for conversation, looking out the window at the young trees bending against the clear sky.

This is the day the Lord hath made, said Mrs. Cherry, swiveling the lipstick and snapping it shut. Rejoice and be glad in it.

Mae nodded. Hallelujah, she said dryly.

Mrs. Cherry walked to the window beside Mae. Mrs. Huff, may I ask if you and your husband are regular churchgoers?

Mae had to take a step back to keep clear of Mrs. Cherry's candy-striped bosom. Well we used to go to the Methodists, she said. Don't much any more.

I wonder if you'd be interested in attending my church. Mrs. Cherry fished in her patent-leather purse and came up with a pamphlet. Here, you can read all about it.

THE GOOD NEWS TABERNACLE was printed in red capitals, beneath the picture of a throne. It might have been mistaken for an armchair except for the crown suspended above it and the ring of short lines to indicate radiance.

Now I want you to promise me you'll come to worship with us, said Mrs. Cherry. I simply will not rest until you do.

Well now I can't make no promises, said Mae. Lionel, he likes his sleep of a Sunday.

The lures of the tempter are many, said Mrs. Cherry. Can anyone survive without the strength of the everlasting arms?

She looked as if she expected an answer. Well, I'll read this, said

Mae, tapping the pamphlet against a flowerpot.

Good, said Mrs. Cherry. There is rejoicing in heaven. She left and the wind slammed the door after her.

Mae sat heavily in the rocker and picked up the pamphlet. The print was blurred, the type face grown blunt as an old dog's teeth. The letters sloped a little on the page.

> Is yours also a broken life? Every life out of harmony
> with God is an unsatisfactory one. If you will receive
> Jesus Christ as your saviour, God has a wonderful
> plan for YOU.

Mae put it down and did not read any more. The words made her uneasy, as if she'd done something that meant bad luck. But if she didn't read it she was doing exactly what they warned about. Stop it, Mae told herself. A damned old fool she was to get jumpy over a stupid piece of paper. She stood up and latched the front door open so the fresh air blew in. She was just nervous and needed to get her mind off things.

The bright day made her wish she was outside. Maybe she would go for a drive, not to pick things up, just a drive. The idea pleased her. She pushed back the curtain. Lionel, she called. Watch things for me. I'm going out. She heard him say something from behind the bathroom door. Mae tied a scarf over her head and slipped out the back.

The keys were already in the ignition and in less than a minute she was on the highway. The dusty glass made the sun glare, so she rolled the window down. She passed farms, the bare fields not yet plowed. Nobody wanted to start too early and get washed out in the rains that could turn the ground to thick soup. The farmers met in groups at the gas station or hardware store, shifting their weight from one foot to the other, talking about last spring's weather, what the long winter might mean, how soon it would be safe. It was an uneasy time of year for them. But the weather hurt everybody, made them expect too much and feel too bad when things went wrong.

The more Mae thought about Mrs. Cherry's church the more she was convinced she wanted no part of it. She could picture it: a frame building isolated in a gravel parking lot. It would be too hot or too cold inside and the chairs would be deliberately uncomfortable and the people would all say things like Praise God every other minute. She didn't trust folks who were liable to talk in tongues or fall to the floor gibbering. She had too much sense for that.

Of course she believed in religion and all. There was just no reason to get hysterical about it. Mae had a sudden vision of herself, kneeling awkwardly on a bare wooden floor, rocking back and forth. No, she could never do it.

It was time to head home. Maybe she and Lionel should put in a garden, she thought, looking at the bright sky. It always felt good to start a garden this time of year.

Hand-painted china, said Mrs. Cherry. Not the patterned kind.

Mae stood on a chair to reach the top shelves. The weather had turned sullen and she wore her old sweater again. Mrs. Cherry had a coat with a dark fur collar; it made her face look pale and shrouded.

There's this pitcher, an a set of teacups an a platter, said Mae. She avoided looking at Mrs. Cherry. Why should she feel guilty because she didn't go to that silly church? Wasn't it her own business?

Why don't you look through these, said Mae. I'll see if I can find some more. Mae rummaged among the Mason jars and china figurines, moving briskly from one shelf to the other. She was aware of Mrs. Cherry standing motionless behind her.

I guess that's it, said Mae. One foot at a time she stepped from the chair to the floor, then polished the seat of the chair with a dish towel. Mrs. Cherry turned the platter around and around in her hands. How much for this, she asked.

Two fifty, said Mae. She could have asked for a dollar more but she was anxious to avoid any argument.

Mrs. Cherry held out two ones and a half-dollar. See, said Mae, taking the coin and throwing it into a desk drawer, I save those, don't get to spend them. It's like you're getting it for two dollars.

I should be so lucky, said Mrs. Cherry. But you don't get something for nothing.

That's the truth, said Mae. She waited for Mrs. Cherry to say good-bye. Instead she turned and looked out the window, through the lampshades with dangling glass prisms, the bud vases, and cracked toasters. Her hands were in her pockets and it drew the fabric tight across her broad hips. God, thought Mae, I hope I don't ever get quite that fat.

Mrs. Huff, do you know the dangers of worldliness? Mrs. Cherry spoke without turning around.

Beg pardon?

If our hearts are filled with the Lord Himself, our love for the things of the world shall wane. The voice seemed to come from the coat instead of Mrs. Cherry.

I'm not sure I know what you mean, said Mae. She was frightened. People didn't talk like this.

Mrs. Cherry turned from the window and the tight sausage curls on her forehead quivered. The things of the world, Mrs. Huff. The lust of the flesh and the lust of the eyes and the pride of life is not of the Father, but is of the world. And the world passeth away, and the lust thereof: but he that doeth the will of God abideth forever.

Her voice was somber. She shook her head sadly, picked up the platter and went out the front door. Mae watched her walking on tiptoe around the mud puddles. She felt relieved she'd left, but also angry, as if she'd been unjustly accused of something.

You know that Mrs. Cherry, she told Lionel at supper. She's kind of strange.

Lionel mopped up his plate with a slice of bread. All those jumping Jesus people are strange. All of em got holy water in place of brains.

Mae giggled. But that wasn't the way she felt about Mrs. Cherry. Mrs. Cherry made her feel sad, kind of, sad and upset and she didn't know why. Hey, she said. Does Mr. Cherry go to church with his missus?

Lionel shrugged. Don't know. Doesn't seem like he'd be able to what with running three stores. Those church people want you praying full-time.

I guess it makes them happy, said Mae. She pushed herself up from her chair and stacked the dishes in the sink. But, she told herself, it didn't seem to make Mrs. Cherry happy.

The phone's dull ring was like marbles rolling across a sheet of tin. Mae felt it invade her sleep, pulling her eyes open. Christ, she said, and sat up. The familiar room took on new angles in the darkness; she banged her knee against a table reaching for the phone. Hello, she said, and the silence in the receiver was like darkness too. Hello, she said again.

Mrs. Huff? The voice was breathy and uneven.

Who's this?

Mrs. Huff, will you come see me?

What, said Mae. I can't hear you. Who's this?

Mae, called Lionel from the bed. What's going on?

I can't hear, said Mae. Who is this?

Louise.

I don't know no Louise. What the hell is this? Her fright was turning to anger. She groped along the wall and turned on a light. The clock said 1:30.

This is Louise Cherry, the voice said.

Oh, said Mae. She could say nothing more. She turned from Lionel, mouthing questions at her, and stared at the blackness of the window.

I want you to come see me at home, said Mrs. Cherry.

Right away, said Mae. Right away. She hung up the phone but did not move.

What's wrong, said Lionel. He was sitting up in bed; his voice was petulant.

Nothing, said Mae, and took her clothes into the bathroom to dress. In the glare of the fluorescent tube she saw her face, heavy and creased from sleep, her rumpled hair. She walked to the hall and took her coat off its hook.

Where are you going?

To see Mrs. Cherry. Go back to sleep. She left him staring at her, his mouth open and slack. She didn't want to explain things, didn't want to talk about why it seemed right she should be up in the middle of the night, leaving her house because someone told her to. That was it. She had been ordered to do it. It didn't make sense but she knew she had to go.

No one was on the streets. Even the stoplights had been turned off for the night. The truck rattled and coughed, and Mae felt strange thinking that for all its noise no one heard it. She knew the Cherry house, a two-story brick with white pillars, supporting nothing, on the front. Mae parked in the driveway and the gravel crunched under her feet.

She knocked and the door swung open under her hand. Mrs. Cherry, she called. There was no answer. An upstairs light threw a path of soft yellow down the staircase in front of her. Mrs. Cherry? Mae closed the door behind her. The carpet under her feet was thick and yielding. The rooms on either side were dark but she sensed the gleam of polished wood, the airiness of the high ceilings. Mae climbed the stairs, her feet leaving soft indentations in the carpet. When she got to the top a voice said In here.

A low, pink-shaded lamp made the room seem small and hot. Mrs. Cherry lay full-length on the bed, dressed in a blue quilted dressing gown. She stared at Mae as if she didn't know her. Then her mouth twitched and she raised herself on one elbow. The light has come into the world, she said, and men loved darkness rather than light, because their deeds were evil. She nodded, as if daring Mae to contradict her.

Mrs. Cherry, said Mae, are you here all alone? Where's your husband?

Mrs. Cherry began to cry, swaying back and forth so the bed bumped rhythmically against the wall. She cried with her mouth open and choking noises came from her throat.

Now don't cry, said Mae. She noticed a heavy smell in the air, like decaying flowers. Jungle Gardenia and gin, she figured. Mae sat on the edge of a chair and after a while Mrs. Cherry grew quiet. She rubbed her nose with the back of her hand and stared at Mae with fierce, red-rimmed eyes.

Mae looked away. She felt she should say something. A real nice house you got here.

Mrs. Cherry began crying again. Now I didn't mean it, said Mae. I mean—she gave up and let her hands fall to her sides.

Mrs. Cherry spoke, her face muffled in a pillow. I'm a sinner.

Mae wasn't surprised to hear it. Wasn't that what the church folks always said?

A sinner and a hypocrite, said Mrs. Cherry, sitting up. The lust of the flesh holds me.

Oh come now, said Mae, embarrassed. She wasn't sure if that meant . . .

Things! cried Mrs. Cherry. I am snared by the things of the world. With her fingertips she picked at the fabric of her dressing gown, glared at the blue silk as if it were the foulest of filthy rags. Vanity and waste!

Now Mrs. Cherry—

Louise.

Louise—an you can call me Mae, OK?—maybe it's none of my business, but I came all the way over here and I might as well tell you what I think. You're upsetting yourself for no good reason. It's no crime to want nice things. If it were, nobody in the county wouldn't be behind bars. An if you don't cheat nobody to get your money, nobody begrudges you buying things, least of all me. Why, I'd be a damned fool not to want your business. Mae sat back in her chair, convinced by the common sense of her argument.

Mrs. Cherry rolled over on the bed, twisting and straining to get under the sheet. The process suggested laundry billowing on a clothesline. When nothing of her was visible but her pink face and snarled hair, she spoke: Verily, verily, it is easier for a camel to pass through the eye of a needle than for a rich man to enter the Kingdom of Heaven.

Mae could not contain her exasperation. As long as I'm telling you what's on my mind I might as well tell you all of it. Louise—Mae was careful with the name—you're letting this religion thing get to you. It's not supposed to ruin your life or anything. I know plenty of folks who're Christians and they don't let it bother them one bit. Why can't you just relax about it?

Oh the seed which is planted on shallow ground, Mrs. Cherry

answered sadly. Each believer that falls away is another wound in the Sacred Heart. True faith gives peace but not complacency.

Mae got up from her chair and paced the narrow limits of the room. From beyond the heavy blackness of the windows came the sounds of the year's first crickets and frogs. OK, she said. I'm going to try one more time and I hope you'll give me an answer I can understand. Why did you call me out here if you're not going to listen to a word I say?

Mrs. Cherry drew the sheet up to her nose. The bed clothes convulsed. She had shrugged her shoulders. Why did you come, she asked.

Mae stopped her pacing. It was hard to answer. It had made more sense when she was half-asleep. It was a command, that was part of it. And it had something to do with her own restlessness, the notion that Mrs. Cherry could fix it for her. Or rather, she would find out what was bothering Mrs. Cherry and fix it for them both. Mrs. Cherry's eyes, very blue and somehow vulnerable, were on her. Suddenly it seemed imporant to make her happy. But Mae said only I figured you needed help.

After a moment Mrs. Cherry sighed and sat up in bed. Well you're right about one thing, she said. Her voice was calmer. Thinking about the church upsets me. I've been ashamed to go there lately, knowing I preach one way and practice another. But you can help me. If you really want to.

Mae imagined what would come next. Kneeling next to Mrs. Cherry until sun-up, Mrs. Cherry's heavy breath filling the air as she intoned loud and tearful prayers. Inwardly Mae sighed. Sure, she said. Sure I'll help you.

Mrs. Cherry swung her legs over the edge of the bed. I want, she said, groping for a belt loop, I want you to help me get rid of my worldly goods.

You mean you're giving everything away? In spite of herself Mae's eyes strayed to a little gold clock on the dressing table.

No! Mrs. Cherry was on her feet by now. She looked more like her old self, authoritative, bustling. I want to destroy all of it. With your help.

But Louise. There's poor people who could use your things. It'd be at least as much of a sin to throw them away. Mae hoped her argument didn't sound stingy. She wasn't talking about herself and Lionel, they weren't charity cases. Still, there were things nobody else would want, nobody, that they could fix up and sell . . . Mae tried to put the idea out of her head. This would be harder even than praying all night.

We will destroy only useless, vain articles that would tempt people, Mrs. Cherry replied. Already she was rummaging through dresser drawers.

But . . . Well, how are you going to do it?

Burn them. Bury them. I don't care. Dump them in the reservoir. We can use your truck.

All right, said Mae, how about Sunday afternoon? You decide what you don't need, I can pick up a load—

I have to do it tonight, said Mrs. Cherry, straightening up and glaring at Mae. Her insistence turned plaintive, tears once again making her eyes glassy. If I don't do something when the spirit moves me—something sincere—I may never have the strength again.

Have it your way, Mae said. She and Mrs. Cherry gathered laundry baskets, garbage cans, plastic sacks. Mrs. Cherry ripped pictures from the walls, smirking china statues from the shelves. Bright streams of jewelry ran into the baskets. Perfume atomizers, Frank Sinatra records, ashtrays: the pile grew. In the kitchen, its white Formica counters drifting like ice floes in the blue tile of the floor, Mrs. Cherry collected a toaster cover, ornamental plaques, a French cookbook. From the refrigerator she took a dark, moisture-beaded jar and nodded with special significance at Mae as it dropped onto the heap. Caviar, she said.

Mae set to work hauling the full baskets out to the truck. In spite of her resolve she was not happy. She recognized some of her own sales in the pile, and she couldn't help toting up the value of the things Mrs. Cherry was throwing out. From the hall she heard Mrs. Cherry upstairs, a steady noise of small metallic collisions. Mae reached out and touched a lace tablecloth, its fine threads crisp and delicate. Crazy as a goony-bird, she said under her breath. Wish I could afford stunts like this. But she took the tablecloth out to join the rest.

By the time they were ready to go the sky was milky, marbled with the coming day. Mrs. Cherry still wore her bathrobe. I'd renounce it too, she said, except I don't feel like changing right now. The unsteady load of fine things looked strange against the battered green sides of the truck. On top perched an enormous straw hat trimmed with artificial grapes; Mrs. Cherry had placed it there as carefully as if she had been packing it in tissue paper. Mae backed the truck out of the drive. Where to, she asked.

The gravel pit, said Mrs. Cherry. Her face was calm and plump. She did not look like a woman who had been up all night. The rest of it, she said, I intend to sell at a garage sale. I'll give the money to the cancer people.

They drove in silence through the town, its streetlights pink and waning, onto the main highway. A warm breeze stirred the wet grass; another fine day that might mean spring. Each noise from the back of the truck angered Mae, pulled at her good resolutions. That was money being thown away. It wasn't helping anybody. And if Mrs. Cherry happened to get certified crazy, she, Mae, would get mixed up in it too. Why hadn't she talked Mrs. Cherry out of it? Maybe it wasn't too late. It wouldn't hurt things to sit out in the open a day or so if Mrs. Cherry changed her mind later. Now tell me, said Mae. Do you feel better for doing this?

Mrs. Cherry nodded. It's an act of faith, she said, and hesitated, fingers absently stroking her sleeves. It's the right thing to do. Don't you think so? I mean, you don't think I'm falling into the sin of false humility?

Mrs. Cherry's questions rose, wavered in the air. The blue of her eyes turned purple, bruised. Oh no, said Mae hurriedly, don't worry about it. After another mile Mae tried again. Tell me, she said. Do you think it'd be right for me to clear out my store? Just dump everything?

Mrs. Cherry considered this. No, she said, it's how you earn your daily bread. For you it's no sin, having things. But Mae—and Mrs.

Cherry too was timid with names—it was you who gave me strength. I never could have done it without you. You are an instrument of God's plan.

Mae winced, but turned her face to the window so Mrs. Cherry could not see. When they reached the gravel pit the sun was streaking the sky with strips of red and white, like a slab of bacon. Its rays touched them with fiery light, made a ring of brightness around Mae as she stood, grim but efficient, cracking a pile of saucers in half.

The People of Color

Behind two sealed panes of glass, and screened by the low branches of Norwegian pine, they felt quite safe watching. Not that there was much to see. A U-Haul truck parked in the driveway, full of lamps, folded quilts, rugs, cardboard boxes squared away on the back wall—perfectly ordinary.

What did you hope to see, David said. Dildoes? A mummy case?

Very funny.

Firearms. Half a dozen enema bags.

I'm just curious, said Meg. She folded her arms as if they could serve as a barrier to his teasing, though she knew he wouldn't stop yet.

Maybe this truck is just a fake and the real stuff, the good stuff, will be smuggled in under cover of darkness.

Yeah. You want the first watch?

But David's amusement was still private. He sat slumped over the table, his neck pouched and foreshortened, elbows dug in. His chin was ragged with black whiskers, each one distinct as a mole.

You've got to admit it, he said. You're really nosy. A voyeur. That means—

I know what it means. You need a shave.

At age sixty you and your fellow crones, your crone cronies, will hold long telephone conversations about some poor wretch's laundry hanging on the line.

You also need a haircut.

The last one looked like it was done with pinking shears, leaving little tufts and eruptions of hair along his neck. He didn't answer, of course, just kept on talking in his voice that was always hoarse yet always projected more than it needed to. A voice that was used to speaking with authority. It was one of the things she accommodated, this insistence on his own humor that left her behind, just as she had resigned herself to his occasional snoring. He was such a clever man, a real original. Everyone said so, and his demonstrable intelligence made one make allowances. He kept talking until the joke was brought to some peak or challenge she no longer followed. He grinned, waiting for her answer. His cheeks were always a bright inflamed red, as if they'd been scoured.

Meg said All we know is that people of color have furniture just like white folks.

It was not an answer and he had to visibly shift gears. Huh. Yeah, here they are again.

She looked but the angle of the house obscured them. Two figures in matching army jackets and jeans. Nearly the same height. She couldn't tell which was the man. They all look alike. The joke was stillborn. Wind drove the pine branches down, then they bucked, swung up, like a log riding waves. Through the shifting green she saw them unloading the truck; one, the woman maybe, handing things down to the other, until the ground was bright with pillows, record albums, clothes sagging from hangers. Meg looked at her own table, the patterned blue china, graceful even though littered with the remains of their breakfast, the salt and pepper, back to back in their place at the center, the blue glossy field of vinyl tablecloth. She felt a small innocent contentment at the harmony of what she saw, at the thought that her belongings were not scattered on that cold mud.

David was saying something. Beg pardon, she said, raising her eyes.

I said if they eat on their porch we'll be able to exchange plates. He nodded at the enclosed porch, much like their own but not quite parallel, attached to the white frame house some six yards away.

The McAllisters never did.

Maybe not.

Besides there's all this vegetation. The longest pine needles probed the glass as she spoke. I think life will go on.

I guess. You don't suppose there'll be any ruckus because they're black.

Meg shook her head. The front part of her hair worked itself loose from the rubber band holding it back, two heavy red wings already starting to frizz. No burning crosses. Maybe a little ostracism. I should bake a cake or something, take it over.

That would be liberal of you.

David I'd bake a cake for anyone, you know—She saw by his grin that he'd tricked her.

Will it be a chocolate or a vanilla cake?

Very funny. She spoke primly, trying not to laugh.

Talk about knee-jerk responses. He stood up and his unbalanced chair teetered.

Don't you dare. He was standing over her. His loose work shirt made his body seem massive, undefined. His hands were flexed and ready.

David!

She squirmed within the folds of her old green bathrobe. His shoulders dropped until they were level with her head, his hands prying hers loose. She whooped when he felt for her ribs, then bent double as her laughter came in spasms. Finally he lifted her out of her chair, holding her by her armpits while her heels skidded against his legs.

She couldn't speak for a full minute after he put her down. Her eyelashes were matted, damp. She reached up, kissing him. You big bully.

He blew in her ear. And what will the neighbors think?

She put the breakfast dishes to soak and got out her mixing bowls. It'll be a coffee cake, she called to David, but he must have been in the back of the house. Sprawled on the unmade bed reading, most likely. He had a way of taking up the maximum possible space. You couldn't forget for a minute that he was in the house. He left a trail of clothes, books, overflowing ashtrays; his footsteps made glasses ring on the shelves. A clumsiness, an obtrusiveness she associated with men in general and did not allow herself to nag about. Nagging was for *hausfraus*, knee-jerk liberals, broads on TV commercials who fretted about waxy build-up. She had promised herself right at the start of her marriage never to submit to such self-images.

As always she fell into the rhythm of the baking. Her nostrils filled with the smell of sweet dough. The polished blue sky and sun were deceptive. It was only March, and the heat of the oven felt good on her bare legs. If you looked into the heart of the pine tree so you saw just a corner of sky and fat cloud, then you might fool yourself into thinking the weather was nice.

Meg dressed, squinting at herself in the bathroom mirror. She looked like a war orphan this morning she thought, pale as the soap in the dish. Even her freckles were faded. She shrugged off the idea of makeup, covered the cake with a clean dish towel, and walked across the lawn.

She knocked. Blurred noise came from behind the door—heavy feet, the wrench of furniture, thin high music. She knocked louder. The door opened as she raised her hand a third time.

It was the woman. Light skin, beige with an undertone of gold, and short kinked hair worn natural. Yes, she said.

Meg hoped she wouldn't sound too rehearsed. Hi, I'm Meg Macey and I live next door. I wanted to ask if there was anything I could do to help you get settled, and I brought you a little coffee cake.

Oh, said the woman, surprised and tentative. Meg lifted the dish towel. Why it looks homemade. Meg nodded. And it's still *warm.* Her voice was soft, breathy. Well that's awful nice of you. Hey come on in.

I don't want to get in your way, began Meg, but the woman had already swung the door open and stepped inside. The music came from a stereo already set up in the corner, a bright falsetto soul record. Verg, the woman shouted. Verg, c'mere. A voice answered but all Meg caught was the tone, heavy and irritated. I don't care, the woman called. She turned to Meg and smiled. He'll be out in a minute. He's havin a fit with the shower curtain. Here, you want to set that plate down? The woman dusted a cardboard box with her shirt sleeve. Oh, I'm Esther. Esther Billups. Did you say Meg? Have a seat. Somewheres.

Esther spread her arm over the uneven terrain of the room, the disassembled bookcases and toppling piles of clothes. She produced two vinyl couch cushions and Meg sat, cross-legged, Esther stooped to turn down the music. She was tall, maybe five ten. Long slim legs and narrow waist. In her middle twenties, probably, though Meg always found it hard to tell black people's ages. Esther's eyes were very large, almond shaped. Looking at the strong curves of her cheekbones, her wide forehead and full mouth, Meg realized that despite the old clothes, despite the brown skin that somehow qualified all her perceptions and put them in a separate category, Esther was beautiful.

Esther plumped down on the other cushion. So you live in that house yonder? The one just like ours?

Well they're not quite alike. Our living room's bigger, and you've got an extra bedroom.

That so? They look exackly alike from the street you know. Like twins.

I guess, said Meg. Secretly she thought her own house, with its evergreens and brick walk, was much nicer. Did you move from out of town, she asked.

Esther shook her head. No, we were living out west but we needed a bigger place. A wadded newspaper in the corner rustled and produced a skinny gray kitten which ran to Esther, butting against her ankles and mewing. Esther picked it up. Cat, what did I ever do to you besides give you a home? Then she twisted her neck around, hearing footsteps behind her. Bout time, she said to the man who apeared in the door frame.

He scowled. Where's the hammer, he asked, not looking at Meg.

Now how would I know? You packed it. Verg, this is Meg— Macey.

Meg Macey from next door an she brought us a cake, ain't that nice? This my husband Verg.

Meg could see the man struggling to keep his ill humor intact. How do, he said. He was darker than Esther, his features bunched too close together. Maybe it was the frown that lowered his forehead. He was wearing a T-shirt and his bare arms bulged with angular muscles. I need that hammer, he said. No way I'm buyin a new one. He stood for a moment longer, his suppressed anger making him rock a little on his feet, then he turned and disappeared.

Grouch, said Esther without embarrassment. But Meg was already on her feet. I better not keep you from your unpacking, she said, for once glad to use a polite formula. Is there anything you need?

Naw. Just takes time is all. Hey thanks for the cake, that was sure thoughtful of you. Esther stood up and stretched, her long legs growing taut. The kitten spilled from her lap. Drop on by again, you hear? We can have a beer or somethin.

She's real nice, Meg told David at dinner. He's kind of a character.

David put his milk glass down, swabbed at the smeared moustache it left. A character?

Not very friendly.

Well I guess we don't have to be great buddies. Just not get in each other's way. Hope they don't throw wild parties.

We might get invited.

And have you ogled by a crowd of jive-talking bucks? Uh uh.

You could tie me to your wrist with the clothesline, Meg said, trying to keep her voice mild. This mock protectiveness was somehow irritating.

C'mon Meg, don't sneer.

You sound like a caveman.

What's wrong with that? Rescuing you from a crowd of dusky ravagers. It turns me on. He beamed, thinking of new jokes. Where is that clothesline, go get it, will ya?

Holy shit, Macey, there's cops and niggers all over your front yard.

Meg struggled to sit up in the back seat where she'd been asleep, her body reacting to the words before she was conscious of them. Between David and Clark's shoulders she saw a wedge of darkness and

the mute explosion of red flashing lights. Christ, said David. What
did they do, rob a bank?

The car approached, rolling, nearly silent, and the scene resolved
itself into components: two policemen getting into a patrol car,
backing into the street and racing away even as they watched, two
more in the yard, standing on each side of Verg Billups, another
writing on a clipboard by the light of the street lamp. Clark pulled
into the driveway and they all got out, uncertain of what to do.

Should we inquire, asked David, turning to Meg. She shivered,
the night air penetrating her clothes, and didn't answer. David
shrugged and walked away toward the policeman with the
clipboard.

How long have they lived here, asked Clark.

Only a week, no, ten days. She was watching Verg, who stood
looking at the ground. The red beam cut across his face as it re-
volved, pulsing every other second, so his features seemed to alter-
nately leap and smolder. But from this distance she couldn't read
them.

David jogged back across the frozen grass. Domestic disturbance,
he reported, wheezing. He knocked her around some.

Meg breathed cold night air, felt her lungs stop. Esther—how is
she?

I dunno, I didn't, hey Honey—

But she broke away from his arm before it could encircle her, and
trotted across to the policeman. He looked up, his face tinged with
blue from the stark light, his voice weary and courteous. Yes
ma'am?

Where is Mrs. Billups, will she be all right?

Well I think so ma'am. She's at the hospital but she seems just
bruised, shaken up. No weapons in the assault.

What happens—what happens—She wanted to ask him what
would happen to the two of them, Esther and Verg, what would they
do? Of course he couldn't tell her, and he was waiting patiently for
her to realize it.

We'll see if she presses charges. He nodded in Verg's direction: he
was being loaded into the back of a patrol car. If she doesn't sign a

complaint against him we can't do anything. The man smiled, dismissing her.

She told him good-night and walked away. Guess I better move on, Clark was saying. You folks rest easy. She let David say good-night for her, let him lead her into the house. After the darkness the lights seemed too bare, distinct, each object harshly defined and unfamiliar.

I'll be damned, said David. There goes the neighborhood, huh?

Oh don't. Don't joke.

I didn't mean anything, Meg.

I know. She walked across the room, picked up something, a book, put it back down. I would never, she said, her voice surprising both of them, never stay with a man who beat me.

Wow! His laughter stuttered, then failed altogether. Wow, is that a warning? You think I'd ever hit you, you're crazy.

I know. Forget it. She saw him hesitate, then decide to say something casual. You want a drink of something, a nightcap?

Sure, she said, and crossed the room to him, pressing the warm length of her body to him until he put his arms around her.

They had two drinks, stayed up later than they meant to until they felt their earlier fatigue return to them. Still Meg couldn't fall asleep right away. She drew back the covers, knowing she would not disturb his heavy sleep, and crouched at the bedroom window. But the house next door was dark, giving no sign of anyone within the blank walls.

When Meg awoke the memory of the night before was like a sharp edge, something she had to blunt with her morning routine, the familiar actions assuring her that whatever happened could be assimilated, dealt with. Perhaps even forgotten, or turned into an anecdote: Honey you remember when the neighbors had that fight? But at noon someone knocked on the door. She was not really surprised to see Esther.

Good morning, Meg said, hating the inane brightness of her voice.

Mornin. Hey, can I use your telephone? Mine was sposed to be in yesterday, wouldn't you know. Yeah, thanks, preciate it.

Meg held the door open and showed her where the phone was. Trying not to be obvious, she examined Esther for damage. Nothing she could see. Esther wore a bright purple scarf wrapped sleekly over her head. It made her look like a statue of some Egyptian queen.

Esther spoke into the phone, a few words in her soft voice. Meg stood in the next room, a polite distance that would show she wasn't trying to eavesdrop. When she heard the phone click she returned.

Well thanks again, said Esther. Hope I didn't put you out none.

Of course not, said Meg. Come over whenever you need to call. Was she imagining it, or was there something constrained, hesitant in the way Esther spoke. Meg let her impulse break loose: Hey are you all right? After last night I mean?

She was ready for Esther to say it was none of her business. Instead she raised her arms, let them drop heavily to her sides. Yeah. Yeah, I'm OK. Got a sore ass and a headache.

Would you like something, some coffee?

Coffee'd send me into orbit. I'm kinda edgy, you know.

How about some dope then?

They were sitting at the kitchen table surrounded by a comfortable clutter of ashtrays, Pepsi bottles, vanilla wafers, thick rising smoke. We made it up, Esther was saying. She spoke with difficulty, trying to hold the smoke in her lungs. He was pissed I called the cops, I never done that before.

You mean he hit you before? The dope had made Meg hazy, incautious. But it was all right.

Couple times he gave me a punch. Oncet he kicked me upside the head.

Wow! Meg didn't trust herself to say more. But Esther must have caught the disbelief.

Girl, you gotta know I light into him too. Threw a dozen eggs at him one time. Mashed a couple down his shirt.

Yeah, but—Meg shook her head, stopped. There was no way she could say what she felt. That it was the worst degradation to put up with such abuse, and any woman who did had her brains scrambled.

He just gets so mad, said Esther, ignoring the interruption. Her brown eyes slid upwards, remembering. Mm, does he get mad. Allus been like that, we been married a year but I've know him for three. How long you been married?

Two years in June. Meg felt oddly embarrassed, as if talking about her marriage, its normalcy and lack of violence, was boasting.

But Esther didn't seem uneasy. A June bride, huh.

Oh sure. The works. Made my folks happy. Meg giggled. We were so cute. Like the little bride and groom they put on the wedding cake. A lu-uvly couple, she drawled.

What's your old man do?

He's a creative consultant for a public relations firm.

Huh. Ole Verg is just public. He drives trucks for the city.

They both laughed. Esther rummaged through the cookie box. Am I ever bein a pig. But this is ba-ad weed. It took Meg a minute to figure out that bad meant good. I didn't know white people had weed like this.

Yeah, it's OK stuff, said Meg. She thought, vaguely, that blacks must know more about whites than vice versa, just because they had to live in a world where whites made the rules. For the same reason women must know more about men than men do about women. Was that right? She'd have to remember it, think about it when she got straight. Her general curiosity triggered a specific question. Esther, she asked, how old are you?

Twenty-four. Twenty-four last November.

Why me too. Except I was born in August.

Huh, I'd a thought you were younger. I dunno why.

The freckles, probably. They make me look like Raggedy Ann.

Hey now I got freckles too, see? Esther leaned across the table and Meg saw it was true, a cluster of darker brown pigment across the bridge of her nose. I've always been proud of em cause it's real unusual for black people to have freckles. An I'm not even that light.

Well you're pretty light, said Meg. Was there something indelicate about her mentioning it?

Esther shook her head. The darker the berry the sweeter the juice, that's what some folks say. But my mamma used to say right back, well damn the berry and fuck the juice, mm-mm.

Meg coughed in her Pepsi, couldn't stop laughing. The bubbles flew up her nose, laugh bubbles. It would be wonderful, she thought, to have a mother who said things like that.

When they both calmed down Esther said Jesus, I got to get home. I must of been here all day.

It was only two-thirty. But Meg felt that they had indeed been there all day, or that they always spent the day like this, something. She staggered a little, her hands swimming as she stood up.

Esther was trying to put her coat on. This thing hasn't got enough sleeves, she complained.

Mine neither. Meg was rooting through the hall closet. Hangers fell in dark rattling piles.

Where you goin?

I have to get some milk before dinner.

Hey, I got milk, plenny of it. Esther seemed pleased to have thought of it. I'll give you some, OK?

They stumbled through the windy sunlight, blinking like owls. Meg was thankful she hadn't tried to go to the store. Esther pushed the front door open. If anything the house was more disordered than the day they'd moved in. Sour piles of clothes lay on the couch. All the shades were drawn and in the yellow dimness Meg put her foot in a saucer of dark dried cat food.

Esther was peering in the refrigerator, both hands on her knees. How much you need, she called. She held out a quart container, half full.

Thanks, that's plenty. I'm going to the grocery tomorrow. I'll pay you back then.

Don't worry bout it. Esther slammed the refrigerator. Ow, I got work to do. Oughta unbraid my hair, had it up since yesterday. She loosened her scarf. Her head was covered with tight braids, giving her scalp a shaved, naked look.

Why do you braid it?

Strengthens it, explained Esther. Makes it easier to handle. I'm not like these gals with foot-wide fros, they got hair you can bounce a ball off of. She reached up and unbraided a section, then bent towards Meg. Feel.

She expected something wiry, stiff. Esther's hair was soft. Like the fleece of a baby blanket. Yeah, said Meg, laughing a little. It's real fine. Esther raised her head and smiled.

I better stumble home, said Meg. Thanks for the milk. I'll pay you back.

I said don't worry, OK? It's a fair trade for the smoke. No, I think I got a real *deal.*

There was something unreal about being at a police station in the afternoon. The atmosphere of crisis, the humming fluorescent lights and cold cinder-block walls required darkness to complete their drama. Instead, the room where Meg and Esther sat was filled with calm sunlight. The blue-green swellings at Esther's eye and mouth seemed as garish and melodramatic as stage makeup.

But, Meg thought, nothing had seemed to fit all day. The incongruity of sirens and pale mid-morning TV screen. Esther staggering across the brown marshy lawn, her awkwardness seeming almost comic, Meg running from her own house just as the patrol car pulled up, all of them asking questions at once so the air filled with peaking voices. The trip to the emergency room where the same TV program droned, imperturbable amid the gauze, alcohol, blood. And now the police station where their tension diffused into a series of reports and forms filled out in triplicate.

Esther was not crying. Only at first, when she ran out of the house, had her voice been thick and liquid. She sat, holding an ice pack to her forehead, her eyes closed. Meg too was silent.

The door to the room opened and Esther's name was called. At the clerk's desk they were told Verg was charged with assault and bail had been set at thirty dollars.

Thirty dollars, said Esther, whispering through cracked lips. He'll be out by dinner time.

Later they sat in Meg's living room. Esther's suitcase was in the corner. She had decided to spend the night with friends, somewhere Verg wouldn't look for her. After that she was unsure.

You have to do something, said Meg. She strained to make her voice firm, as if it alone could change Esther's mind. What are you going to do, wait until he knocks out your teeth instead of just loosening them?

I dunno.

Why not? What's stopping you?

Esther shook her head. It's—hard to decide. I mean, it may sound crazy but I don't want to throw away my whole marriage.

Meg just stared. It was as if she were the one who'd been beaten, humiliated, so intense was her feeling that Verg should be punished. She knew Esther only called the police when it got out of control, she'd said as much herself. How often had she simply endured the violence, or talked her way out of it? Although there was no way Meg could understand such a thing, she realized the extent of the gap between them. When she spoke it was more gently.

You could get a court order saying he couldn't contact you except through your lawyer—what do you call it, a peace bond. It would give things a chance to cool down.

Don't have a lawyer.

Get one.

Don't have no money.

Call Legal Aid. I'll loan you money. Just promise me you'll do something.

Yeah. OK.

Meg heard the gravel in the driveway crush under the wheels of the car. David was home from work. She ran to the kitchen and took the extra house key from its hook. Here, she said, pressing it into Esther's motionless hand and speaking rapidly. If anything happens you come over here, whether or not we're home. Now, we'll give you a ride to your friend's.

She stood on the front porch watching David slump out of the car, his tired after-work gestures. Why, she wondered, had she not wanted David to know about the key. She had known without thinking about it that he wouldn't approve.

Later, he said Why do you think? You might get hurt. Verg might get mad at you for helping Esther.

And then you'd have to do something. You feel responsible for me, right?

She saw his eyebrows tense, saw his hands stiffen on the steering wheel, and knew she was being provocative, unfair. Everything about him grated on her, for no good reason. His too-loud voice, the stale salt odor of his skin. Even his tolerance of her (for she knew he was considering what she'd been through, was making allowances for her mood) irritated her. It smacked of indulgence.

They reached the house. Meg resolved to calm down. But her nerves as she fixed dinner were brittle. David came up behind her, kissed her neck. She tried to respond but some part of her would not relax. Even at dinner when he paid her some over-hearty compliment, transparent in his desire to please, she noticed only the skin of his jaw where the razor had burned and nicked.

Later, soaking in the bathtub, she tried to figure it out. There was no good reason for being mad at David, he hadn't beaten anyone up. He had his moments of insensitivity, of selfishness. What man didn't, they could all drive you crazy. She shifted her legs and the green scented water swirled. She frowned into the tub at her pale body, disjointed by light refracting. She ought to be worrying about poor Esther, not herself.

For the next few weeks Verg Billup's dark figure remained on the periphery of her vision. She'd twist her head, alarmed, but it would be only a drooping pine branch or a swift cloud blotting the sun.

Sometimes, though, it really was Verg. For he and Esther reconciled, fought, talked it over, promised, threatened, then started the cycle once more. Esther seemed to be always in flight, jamming underwear and a toothbrush into her purse, spending the night on sofas and spare beds, never the same place twice or Verg could find her. A lawyer had been consulted, the court order issued, but Esther hesitated to enforce it. She'd talk about divorce; the next day she'd wonder aloud what to get Verg for his birthday. It was a long inconclusive process which wore on Meg's nerves as well. The grass was new and tender, the trees swayed with birds, and they slept with the windows open. But she felt nothing was really changing, just the same endless feud, retreating, then flaring.

Esther had escaped serious injury so far. Perhaps the lawyer had

sobered Verg, though Meg thought him incapable of self-control. The
police had been called twice. Once Verg found the front door locked
and took a tire iron to it. And once Meg watched from her kitchen
through a fine silvery rain as Verg carried out armloads of Esther's
clothes and heaped them in the gutter. A bored-looking policeman in
a rain slicker arrived and made him put them back. When Esther was
away Meg fed the kitten; she moved hurriedly through the dark
kitchen, always expecting to hear Verg's fists splintering the door.

What do they fight about, David asked her. It was a Sunday morning and the floor around him was strewn with newspaper, as if they
were housebreaking a pet.

Meg shrugged. Everything. Nothing. Sometimes I think they enjoy
it. Meg was surprised he mentioned Esther and Verg. His official position had remained that Meg shouldn't get so mixed up in the whole
thing. They seldom spoke of it.

No really. What is there that makes him so violent, or is it just
Verg's sweet disposition?

Well, she said, frowning, he accuses her of seeing other men.

Does she?

Of course not, Meg said. Her voice was a little too heated; she
checked it. Not that she wouldn't be justified, putting up with that
maniac.

You mean he makes up the whole thing? That's hard to believe.

Why? Give other people credit for having imagination.

He stared at her. She thought this was how he confronted people at
work when there was difficulty: eyes level, appraising, his whole body
squaring itself. Verg's talents seem to be more in the manual line, he
said, although he may have hidden executive potential.

You're making an unfair accusation about Esther.

I'm not accusing her. I simply posited that for so much smoke,
there might be a small flame.

Why do you automatically take his side?

If I did, you automatically took hers.

Meg had no answer. She looked down at the floor, where some of
the newspaper had wadded under his chair leg. I guess none of it
makes much sense.

He agreed. The thing that's really zany is why she puts up with him.

Of course that was what she couldn't understand herself, and what Esther couldn't or wouldn't tell her. How often Meg found herself asking it, as if repetition would succeed where reason failed. One warm afternoon they sat in Meg's back yard, their bare feet ticklish in the mild air, not yet used to exposure.

Feels *good,* said Esther, arching her back so her shoulder blades nearly touched. Her slow movements were like a continual effortless dance. She had rubbed baby oil into her skin and it gleamed as if sunlight were trapped beneath its surface. She sighed. Wish we was at a beach.

Yeah. Meg closed her eyes. The darkness was veined with red. A beach in California.

Oregon.

Why Oregon.

Sounds like there'd be less people.

OK, Oregon. Behind her eyes Meg saw blue water and pale sand. She and Esther lay in the center of a wide beach. Nothing moved except the white frill of breaking waves. Even their footsteps had been smoothed away. And Meg, for once, did not sunburn, but toasted to an oiled golden brown.

Won't work.

Huh? Meg's eyes pried open.

I keep seein Verg sneak up behind us.

Meg laughed because she could see him too, peering over a cliff. He carried a spear and wore a grass skirt.

Damn, said Esther. He's everywhere. I guess there's no rest for the wicked.

Oh come on. It doesn't have to be like that. As she spoke their old argument hardened in the air. Esther, you could do so much better than him. You've got so much to offer—

Yeah, I got plenty. Just itchin to give it away. She rolled her hips in a mock bump and grind. I'm a real road worker.

You know what I mean, said Meg, annoyed at the evasion. You could do better.

Well but I didn't.

So try again, you act like you're stuck with Verg til the end of your days.

Listen, said Esther, propping herself up on one elbow. Verg has been my friend, my lover, my husband, and my enemy. That's too much to take lightly.

Meg wanted to say Bullshit, it sounded like such a pat speech, but she didn't. At such times she felt, without knowing why, that their different races lay at the core of the misunderstanding. It was an obstacle she could throw herself against forever without either of them understanding the other.

Don't David give you shit? Esther demanded.

Sure, sometimes.

Well I don't see you packin your bags.

Well he doesn't come after me with a tire iron, for one thing.

They were silent. Meg thought miserably that they both probably felt they'd proved their points. She tried seeing it Esther's way. Was that the only debate between them, how much shit you should take? Where was the dividing line? What would David have to do before she'd feel the situation was intolerable. When did you lose your pride, your dignity. Then she thought about leaving David and her vision went vast and blank as the beach she'd imagined earlier. She'd never considered it, even when she was angriest at him.

As if they both realized that it was a standoff they sighed. The sun was reddening, and the dampness of the ground seeped through the towels. I got to get moving, Esther said. I'm sposed to meet Verg in town for dinner.

Meg knelt and reached for her shoes, determined not to challenge her, not even to try. She watched Esther stooping over the towel. The slumped line of her back seemed to show more fatigue than Esther's words admitted. Esther, she said, you're my friend. Please don't get hurt.

Esther smiled. She seemed almost shy. Don't you neither.

When it happened it had the inevitability of nightmare. Glass broke over and over again, like a waterfall. The scream might have been her own; it rang, echoed in the dark bedroom, hung there, seemed to assume form. Then the sound she had always known she would hear, the long cracking of a gunshot.

They were both shouting before they were really awake, their arms colliding, beating against the darkness. David was saying What — what — what — a hoarse monotone, her own voice not yet able to form words. She blinked, suddenly able to see in the dark. David was out of bed, cursing the furniture and struggling with his clothes. She found her robe and waited until he reached the kitchen. She heard the telephone click, heard him stuttering into it, then ran past him to the front door.

Stay in the house, she heard him scream. The heavy door cut him off. She ran, her bare feet sliding in the wet grass. The house next door lurched and tilted in her vision. Before she realized it she was through the door, calling Esther, Esther, her voice shrinking in the sudden silence.

Esther leaned against the refrigerator, her face hidden in her hands. Meg stopped, afraid to come closer. Then Esther lowered her hands and Meg saw that her eyes streamed tears, not blood. Esther's lower lip rolled under her and she said Aaah. Aaah, almost bleating. Meg looked past her, past the ruined window. In a shallow pool of blood, no larger than a dinner plate, lay the kitten, its fur dark and dripping, mouth drawn back in a rigid grin.

Then David seized her, making her stumble, and behind him the room filled with uniforms, heavy feet. David half-dragged her outside, thrust his face in hers. You could have been killed, did you think of that?

She twisted away as far as his grip would let her, then sagged. A policeman emerged steering Esther before him, trotting toward a car. Get back, a voice shouted, get back, and from behind the house two policemen led Verg Billups, his hands already locked behind him. Meg felt David's hand loosen on her shoulder; she broke free and ran to Verg, her heel sinking hard into his gut, fingers at his face. You fucking nigger, she screamed, fucking nigger, the words scalding her throat. She had never, she realized, spoken more than a dozen words to him. Then she was being pulled away and she struck at all of them, hating her weakness. She knew they were afraid to hurt her and she took advantage of it, using her lowered head to batter them, and when they raised it she spat. Then her arms were pinned behind her and she was on the ground.

Squinting through tears she looked for Esther. She was sitting in the patrol car. Meg tried to call to her but as she did Esther looked up. Again Meg felt her throat burn, knew there was nothing she could say. A current of black air seemed to expand, pushing them apart. Then David helped her to stand and they walked away.

Inside he gulped air, trying to slow his breathing before he spoke. I swear I don't know what's got into you.

She did not answer him but noted, with interest, the scrapes and grass stains on her palms, the hot thread of blood running from some cut inside her mouth. She would regard these wounds as badges, and as preparations for the next assault.

Birds in Air

That part of the country is, within itself,
as unpoetical as any spot of the earth; but
seeing it . . . aroused feelings in me which
were certainly poetry.

Abraham Lincoln

An electric fan sits on the refrigerator: it hums, rotates, billows the edge of the tablecloth. Only when it blows directly on me does it cut the heat from the stove and the heat of the day. Eat some more, says Grandma.

On her flowered tablecloth are cold ham, pickles, potato salad, tomatoes, olives, biscuits, honey, white peaches, corn, cherry pie. It is full summer and we live off the fat of the land.

You have some of that country gravy, down south they call it Mississippi butter, says Grandma.

It is thick white stuff with brown crusty bits in it. No one likes it.

It tastes bad, says my younger brother.

Hush, says my mother.

After dinner we sit hot and overfed in the front room. The furniture is dark wood with hard carved edges. The lamps are massive, pink-shaded, with clustered roses or shepherdesses at the base. I look through the white net curtains at the dusty trees, the leaves hanging down like tongues.

Why don't you kids do something, says my father.

It is hard to connect my father with my grandmother's old photographs. A boy in a sailor suit and Buster Brown haircut; odd, dramatic lighting.

Why don't you go to the dime store, says my father.

Where they sell wallets with little Mexican boys stamped on the leather, Souvenir of Spencer County, Ind., sneezing powder, string ties, china ashtrays consisting of a lady on a toilet, Cool Your Hot Butt In My Old Tub.

We've been there before, says my older brother.

You could go to the Lincoln Village, my father says.

Lincoln didn't live in the reconstructed cabins, with the spinning wheels and plaques and corncob pipes and buckeyes for sale. It was north of here somewhere.

We've been there before too, says my younger brother.

Grandma's quilts are all made by hand, pieced out of cotton and linen, red stars and checks, small faded rows of daisies, candy stripes. Sewn together with good white thread, the edges bound and scalloped. In the back bedroom, shades drawn against the afternoon sun, I run my fingers over their taut surface and whisper the names to myself: Wreath of Grapes, Drunkard's Path, Mexican Rose, Birds in Air.

Grandma comes to the door in her long cotton slip. Too hot to sleep, she says. Too hot to do anything.

She sits next to me on the bed. Looking at these old quilts? I nod. Which one do you like best?

My hand hesitates, reaches out to the Birds in Air. A pattern of triangles, like a thousand small wings, which cross and recross until they seem to lift from the cloth.

You can have it, she says, nodding. Her glasses slip and show a red nick in the skin on each side of her nose.

I think of manners, of the way my mother responds to gifts. Oh *no, I couldn't—*

I mean to will it to you, she says. I won't forget. She pats my shoulder with her brittle hand and leaves the room.

Every year there is the visit to the cemetery. Grandma sits in the front seat in her good blue dress. We drive east along the weedy road from town, slowly, my father pointing.

Here's where Lincoln might have played as a boy, he says.

There's his swing set, says my older brother.

Gray sheds and ponds and shade. The limestone cliffs along the river, chalked over with the names of high schools. Dirt roads that disappear into the green distance. I try to imagine Lincoln here. I try to imagine what was different.

We reach the brick pillars of the cemetery gates. We help Grandma from the car and her light skirt floats in the breeze.

I have no grief. I do not remember my grandfather. The sun is hot on the red clover and dandelion puffs. We stand with her a moment, not speaking. Her name is already on the stone beside his, and the date of her birth. Then the numbers 19, waiting to be rounded into four digits. On my fingers I reckon the number of years she can live without spoiling the stone. I promise myself I will never do that, never fix the limits of my life.

After a while we leave her standing there and walk on the long grass between the graves, looking for odd stones, the finger pointing upward marked Gone to Rest, the scrolls and cherubs above the infant graves. The stones are crumbling and we have a contest to find the oldest one. My mother wins with 1820. In the far corner of the lot my brothers start a game of chase.

On the way back we drive through town, the big car strange on the quiet street, the smell of its vinyl seat in our nostrils. Past the feed store and the grocery. There are roofs built out from the stores over the sidewalks, held up by poles buckling into the street. They make a narrow shade on the baked white cement. Peeling boards and black windows, the painted advertisement for a bank sinking into a brick wall.

Really, whispers my older brother, how can people stand to live here?

I frown, tell him to hush. My father is speaking.

That's the jail, he says. I remember once in a while they used to have a drunk in there and we'd sneak up to the window and try to see him. And here's where Great-aunt Norma lived before she moved to Evansville. I used to work in her garden and she paid me ten cents an hour.

My older brother looks straight ahead, but I know he is talking to me: The story that he walked ten miles because he overcharged a customer five cents, is, of course, apocryphal. There are many places where Dad actually spent the night, or some historical incident occurred, but we must separate fact from legend. I mean, I'd hate to see it all get commercialized.

In the front seat my mother, father, grandmother do not move. Perhaps they have not heard. Again I try to imagine, back a hundred and fifty years when the streets were dirt, the paint fresh, Lincoln, on a hot day such as this, barefoot, riding a mule in from the back woods, thinking this a fine place, a big place, the county seat . . . Now the town is full of old people—men in overalls with chapped pink faces, old women living in a fragile world of cats and nicked china and water-stained rugs. The whole back page of the newspaper is for obituaries. Grandma reads them carefully.

The car pulls up in front of the house. I think for dinner we'll finish off the rest of the ham, says Grandma. And maybe some beans, fresh snap-beans.

Help your Grandma do the dishes, my father says to me.   I don't need any help, my grandmother says, go sit down and watch television.   No need for you to do them all yourself.

You just sit down and let me do them.   Finally I take a dish towel from the cupboard and start drying. My grandmother's hands are soft from the water, like old gum erasers, and shreds of vegetables stick under her fingernails. Her hands move in and out of the thin film of soap on the surface of the water, rinsing the bright sharp prongs of the forks. She has one bad eye, with a stripe of blood crossing the iris and the black pupil always large and vacant. The kitchen light is bug-yellow and glaring and it makes the eye water. I see a thick milky tear stream down her face and tremble on her chin.

Grandma looks up, wipes the tear away with a fierce brush of her sleeve. Now you go, she says, and pushes me away from the sink. Go watch television.

Instead I go to the back bedroom, away from the others. Here there is a picture viewer, a stereoscope, with a wire holder for the cards and a wooden hood that fits over your nose and smells of old hair. The cards are heavy and chipped around the edges: views of Niagara Falls, Roman ruins, the Grand Canyon. The story cards are better, girls in pinafores eloping with country swains, ladies in draperies singing Only a Bird in a Gilded Cage. The two flat identical pictures on the card make one with depth and shape. Old jokes, old songs; for a moment they are almost real.

We take Grandma to see her friends. Old ladies who live in crumbling houses, as if the ivy is pulling them softly back to earth and decay. They have names like Dolly, Anna, Pearl. Bunch of old women who wear copper bracelets to keep arthritis away, says my mother under her breath. She does not enjoy these visits.

When Dolly and Anna sit inside they too use electric fans. But when they sit on the front porch they wave paper-and-stick fans with pictures of the American Eagle and Miss Liberty. I think Dolly's son died in the Great War because there are so many pictures of him in uniform.

They are so old, in the middle of a sentence they drift and dream. Even Grandma knows we can't stay long to talk. They wear shapeless lavender print dresses that remind me of the patches in the quilts. Their houses are full of doilies and rugs made of braided bread wrappers. Anna has saved every greeting card anyone ever sent her in the top drawer of her walnut dresser. Mistletoe and violets, angels, risen Christs For the Coming Year and In Sympathy she spreads for our inspection, and smiles.

How pretty. Yes we will. You take care of yourselves. Good-bye Anna. Good-bye Dolly.

Back in the car my mother exhales, as if she has held her breath the whole time.

Now ain't that pitiful, says Grandma. Poor Dolly can't hardly hear. Don't walk so good either. And she's two years younger than me.

We stop for gas at Elnoe's. Elnoe, who is maybe a man or maybe a woman, I'm never sure, immense arms and chest, a sleeveless shirt and jeans, red cheeks, cropped gray hair. How you all, says Elnoe, grinning, showing two gold teeth. Elnoe's white frame house is just behind the gas pumps. The original second story now rests on the ground, a memory of the river's rising. Back home Grandma has a scrapbook of newspaper clippings about the Great Flood of nineteen thirty-something.

There are picnics on the river. From the high bluff we throw stones; they fall into the muddy edges and the great curve of shining water is unchanged. A fast-moving barge passes, blows its horn, and is gone.

My father squats beside my younger brother and his shoes skid pebbles along the riverbank.

Do you know what that is across the river?

The boy squirms at my father's hand on his shoulder. Kentucky.

That's right. Look, says my father, and his arm reaches out to the water and the haze and the fields on the other shore. Pioneers. Indians.

Uh huh, says my brother, and he runs off to look for snakeskins and dead fish.

The sun sets and the light on the river turns opal, glossy. Grandma locks her thin arms around her knees and says to me Your hair is so pretty, it's like mine when I was a girl. It was my father's pride and joy, whenever company came he'd say Della show them how you can sit on your hair. And he sent off for a bottle of lotion that cost a dollar to make my hair shine.

She laughs, pats her short tight curls. I bet you can't imagine me with long hair.

I laugh and do not answer. Darkness spreads from the trees and the crickets surround us. We gather the silverware, waxed paper, pop bottles, chunks of soaked driftwood my brothers carry up from the beach. You know you could take that quilt with you when you go, whispers Grandma. I won't tell nobody.

No, I say, confused, they'd find out . .

I suppose, says Grandma.

You know what I'd like to do while we're here, says my father, is start a family tree.

My mother is brushing crumbs from the breakfast table. What for, she says. You think you'll find royalty?

More likely find we're all descended from John Wilkes Booth, says my older brother.

We visit Mrs. Crawford. Grandma says she knows a lot about things like that. Her parlor is dim, with old pictures hung too high on the walls. I sit in a scratchy armchair. The room smells of dust, attics, and it makes me sleepy. The tables are piled with parchment charts hand lettered in permanent black ink. Birth certificates. The bound volumes of the County Historical Society, round-cornered books with thin, crackling pages.

Of course I knew your folks, says Mrs. Crawford. Walter's cousin George married my sister-in-law . . . The silver frames of her spectacles glint in the darkened room. The parchment scrapes as she unrolls it. She turns on a lamp. Now, she says, do you know when your grandfather was born? My father shakes his head. Together they bend over the table and their fingers trace the lines, lists, old records.

I let my eyes close. In the warm darkness their voices are small and far away.

Maybe it would be easier, Mrs. Crawford is saying, to start from the other end. Here was a settler in Virginia. If you could follow his descendants . . .

My father takes notes on what Mrs. Crawford says, and puts them in his billfold. They will stay there until the creases of the paper grow worn and soiled. Then he will throw them away.

My grandmother still keeps a desk drawer full of toys for us. Coloring books, rubber balls, airplanes made of balsa wood, pennies in tiny glass jugs. Only my younger brother plays with them now. It is afternoon and I am watching TV, an old I Love Lucy show. The screen is gauzy and flickering in the strong light from outdoors.

Grandma comes to the door and stands with her hands on her hips. She asks me if I want some pop: I got Orange Crush, Cream Soda, Root Beer.   I say no thank you.   Some lemonade? She'd be glad to make it.   No, I'm not really thirsty.

I tell you what, says Grandma. I'm going to take you down to

Lotus's shop, buy you a dress. Maybe a pretty blouse, would you like that?

I see my mother's warning face. Sure, I say.

We walk downtown. The heat from the sidewalk wraps itself around my legs. Now you don't worry about how much things cost, says Grandma. You get anything you like.

The windows of Lotus's shop are streaked with old whitewash. A dozen shapeless, limp dresses hang on the racks. They remind me of a church rummage sale.

Lotus has a thin rouged face and lacquered hair. She pulls a stack of blouses from a shelf—can you take an eight, honey?—and watches as I look through them. They are strange prints, like kitchen wallpaper. Patterns of teakettles, vegetables, geraniums. My hands move slower as I reach the end of the pile. I think I have looked at everything in the store. I hold up the last blouse. Can I have this one? I ask my grandmother. Can I wear it home?

The branches of trees meet overhead. The dirt road is a tunnel, scarcely wide enough for the car. You would not drive in these hills at night.

They call this Owl Town because only the owls live here, says Grandma.

Really? asks my younger brother.

People live here too but you won't see them, says my father.

People who will never be on anyone's census or tax roll. Children who would not know what to say to us if we met them, for they have never seen anyone outside their own family.

The air-conditioning chills the back of my neck. We must keep the windows shut. I squint through the tinted glass and try to penetrate the solid green around us. We are going too fast. At the top of a hill I see a path, a fence. I look back and they are gone, the leaves covering them like water closes over a stone. We must start back. It is almost time for dinner.

The bits of thread and cloth come together into blocks, the blocks form patterns. It is hard to tell where the pattern begins and ends, for it crosses and recrosses. My grandmother dies and the telephone company buys her house. But this is not the end. She has left me the quilt. Her fingers moved along its border as mine do now, locking the stitches in place; it cannot be torn, not ever, it has been made too well.

Perhaps it ends when we are ready to leave. Everyone says good-bye to her at least twice, too loudly. My father starts the car. And she comes running after us with her apron over her face. The house is full of gas, she says, pulling at my father's arm. I smell it everywhere. He goes inside with her and the rest of us wait.

My father comes out alone and gets behind the wheel. It was nothing, he says, nothing at all. The car pulls away and although I can't see her at the window, I turn around and wave.

Dry Spring

I counted the days without rain as if they were a late period: thirty, thirty-one, thirty-two. It was a dry spring and it threw everything off. The first green shoots, surfacing on schedule in thick cracked clay, looked isolated, temporary. A steady wind blew from the west, spraying us with dirt from the unplanted fields and making the house strain in all its joints.

Dennis's desk was upstairs, set against a long east window. From there you could see the old barn where a neighbor kept two shabby, bad-tempered horses, and the line of trees that marked the creek. Dennis used to say the view inspired him. Rural poverty, he'd shrug. It inspires me to get rich and get the hell out. The joke had outlived its usefulness. Every so often, if we had company, new people, he might repeat it. But we'd avoid each other's eyes, a little embarrassed, as if we shared in some deceit.

Besides, that spring his writing, the project he'd undertaken with such ambition, was coming hard. It was nothing he felt like joking about. We seldom discussed it but I could tell from his fits of distraction and glumness. I think he was writing a novel. He even hesitated to label it that, I suspect because the thing kept either unraveling or constricting on him until he wasn't sure what he had. It may seem odd that he never talked about it with me. But as he explained, it wasn't that he thought me incapable of understanding it, just that even a hint of criticism from someone so close would be demoralizing.

I've never tried anything like this before, he told me on one of the
few occasions he opened up about it. We were sitting over the last of
dinner, heavy with meat and wine. Dennis narrowed his eyes as he lit
a cigarette. That is, nothing extended like this. It may sound banal,
but I felt I had to take the plunge, see if I had it in me. I used to
think of creativity as somebody shut up in a room, working at fever
pitch all night. Some force came in and possessed you. Did all the
hard part. He shook his head, marveling.

I sat quite still, waiting for more. Most of all I wondered what he
found to write about, day after day, hunched over those secrect
pages. And, in one of those irrelevant and distracting perceptions, I
noticed for the thousandth time the suggestion of cowlick at his
crown. He had very fair hair, worn short. I was always trying to get
him to grow it, claiming he'd had the same haircut since he was
twelve. It gave him a droll look, like a too-solemn child.

You don't, he continued, really appreciate the labor that goes into
writing til you try it. I mean, I respect even bad books now. So the
thing isn't deathless prose, at least there was some fellow pouring his
soul into it. That counts for something.

Of course it does, I couldn't help saying. I think it's the only thing
that counts. Why let critics dishearten you? You can't please them
all.

His green eyes looked quizzical, then amused, and he reverted to
his usual irony. I shouldn't oppress you with this drivel. He patted
my hand.

In the afternoons when he returned from teaching his classes he
paced the kitchen, sandwich in hand, already abstracted, already, in
a sense, at work. Even his pacing had a precise, military air to it.

So how was school, I asked.

He shrugged, running his tongue over his teeth to get the last bit
of tomato. Hopeless. They weren't listening to a thing I said.

I wondered if he told his students he was a writer, thinking to get
their attention. But no, he would be too shy. So I sympathized. I
gave him some small domestic news, like We're out of soap or The
phone bill came. I fixed him another sandwich to take upstairs. He
stooped to kiss me, then I heard his brisk feet climbing.

Well, I thought, watching the silver bulb of a drip grow on the kitchen tap, what wife hasn't faced this in some form or another. A Man and his Work. A Man and his Dog. A Man and his Drinking Buddies. A Man and Anything but his Woman. The drip fattened and fell. The house was silent except for the door rattling in the dry wind. I understood the situation and I wouldn't brood. I would go for a walk.

We lived perhaps five miles from the nearest town, on a road which split two flat fields like a center part in hair. A few unprosperous-looking houses like our own were scattered on it, standard sagging Midwestern frame. Even on the edge of spring the land had a sullen, exhausted aspect to it. As if yet another seeding, tilling and bearing would push it to its limits. Of course the lack of rain hadn't helped. The new green of the grass was tenuous, like a mist hovering above the ground, and the sky was pale and distant.

I set off for the creek as I always did. And as always the two dogs came bounding up to me, distracted from their own adventures. The small part-beagle and the big dappled pointer with the nervous haunches. They pawed me and trotted ahead, tongues out and eager.

Even in winter the two of them ranged for miles up and down the creek, dragging home huge ancient cow bones or a muskrat so long dead that dust rose from its fur when the pointer dropped it. They had a nose for decay, for unearthing things you thought were safely buried. Their last fresh kill had been just as bad, a chicken owned by some Mexicans down the road. I hurried to hide the evidence, scooping it up in a dustpan. But the chicken, though lifeless, thrashed so violently it kept falling off, reminding me of those party games played with spoons and eggs.

The worn, utilitarian landscape had its own beauty. I picked my way down the bank toward the brisk uncoiling water. The creek was lower than it should have been this time of year, but still more than knee-deep in some places. The flat rocks of the bottom, which in August would bask, green-furred, on the edge of the diminished stream, shimmered far below the surface. The steep slopes gave some protection from the wind, though above me the branches of trees continuously tossed and interlaced. Spring was farther along down here, heavy with buds. Stiff wild grasses and lanky weeds had begun their first growth. I followed the creek for perhaps a mile, then turned back. The dogs were far ahead of me, out of sight. At dinner they would return, exhausted and happy, crusted with rank mud. I passed under the damp-smelling cement bridge that marked the road and emerged on the far side, using the roots of a huge old sweet gum as handholds.

I seldom thought of it, but the tree marked the site of a fatal crash. It happened the year before we moved in. One of our neighbors, a little round man who raised hunting dogs, told us about it. Some sixteen-year-old kid, just broken up with his girlfriend, came off the side road going ninety and missed the curve. Our neighbor was the first to reach the scene. Steering wheel cut his spine like it was string, said the little man, relishing our faces.

Now I circled the tree, passing my hands over the trunk to find the place the car had hit. I found nothing, as if the bark had closed up over the scar. It made me sad to think of that boy. Not just that he was dead, but that he'd died for love and was now forgotten. Whatever grandeur that gesture might have had dwindled into anecdote. Of course I was being sentimental. If the dead boy had it to do over again, no doubt he would prefer to live. And perhaps he had not meant to crash, had only failed to catch the white curve markers in his erratic headlights. Still, I wanted to give him the benefit of the doubt, endow him with the full force of passion.

Perhaps it was the wind battering my ears that kept me from hearing anything sooner, but I whirled at the sound of a snapped twig. Not twenty yards away from me, but on the opposite bank, was a figure. For just the rise of a heartbeat I felt I was swimming my way to the surface of a dream. The boy was a little taller than I expected, dark-haired and solemn. He stood motionless, his thin cotton shirt billowing about him. I remember thinking He looks chilled.

All this, of course, was as sudden as my movement. In the next instant he took his hands out of his pockets and reached for a fishing rod, no longer a wraith. I went from dream to the normal embarrassment of someone caught gaping at a stranger. I wished I had something, like his fishing rod, to justify my presence there, even the yelping dogs. He started down the slope, gave me one blank, almost insolent glance, as boys that age will do. His face was long, heavy-jawed, and rather pale. Then he turned his attention to the slippery clay beneath his feet. I walked quickly away.

Thirty-three, thirty-four. Clouds like tattered fur, too thin for rain, raced across the sky. The newspapers talked drought and calamity, though it was hard to imagine one's physical comfort threatened by lack of rain, let alone one's survival. Our cistern was filled by water trucked in from town. The cupboard held cornflakes, chocolate, tinned shrimp, which I toted up smugly.

I walked out to the barn with a pocket of yellow apples for the horses. Dennis was upstairs working, but I didn't wave for fear of bothering him. Our back lot was full of homely debris: a bathtub the color of Pepto-Bismol, in which was heaped old lumber and bedsprings. A trash barrel, rusted through at the bottom. Last spring we had tried to put in a garden, only to find the yard was full of broken glass from years of dumping. The rake dredged up countless bright chips, like a smile clogged with fillings.

I stood at the gate, inhaling the hot animal smell of the barn. I whistled, and the horses, who knew me by now, came trotting in from pasture. First the big dirty palomino mare, a huge silhouette in the open door, vanishing in the central darkness, emerging to butt against my arm. After her the little gelding, who knew too well he'd be bitten if he approached. I threw his apples to him while the mare snuffled over my hand.

Standing there in the exhausting wind, watching the greedy mare show her teeth to the gelding, I felt myself overcome by the most general and useless sort of melancholy. The kind that seeps into me without warning or cause and is only distracted by overeating, bubble baths, or other self-indulgence. The horses, seeing I had nothing more for them, sauntered away. I leaned against the gate, grappling with my mood.

Perhaps it was the enforced quiet of these afternoons when Dennis worked, tiptoeing around him and his vast anonymous project. It had gone on for months and weary months with no sign of ending. Would anything ever come of it? I was surprised I'd even allowed myself such a thought. Well why not, I argued, my mood leading me on. What have I seen to convince me otherwise? What has he done besides announce his intentions, then apologize for them? Does he have it in him? The gate swayed under my weight. It was unsettling to be thinking like this after my long stint of what I'd thought was sympathy and patience. The most I'd admitted to myself before was a sneaking desire to see my name on a dedication page. To my dear wife. But now I felt, for whatever reason, analytical and distant. Oh, he was a clever man, everyone said so, everyone assumed he could succeed at whatever he attempted. Cleverness and discipline, these he had in abundance. But they were the surface, the rind. Peel them away, as you must—what lay beneath? What did it take to put life on a page, to create anything? I had only vague notions, which I could not put names to, but I thought of Dennis grading papers, his sternness as he read them, his furious exclamatory scribbles. Awkward! Trite! Redundant!

Now I was judging my husband in some vague but implacable way. Perhaps it was jealousy, some crabbed ungenerous part of me that begrudged his effort. I would never wrestle words onto paper. Perhaps we all fear what we are not. Perhaps long intimacy produces such growths on occasion, like outlandish fleshy mushrooms. I thought of Dennis's furtiveness, his fretful defensiveness about his work, and I told myself He has good reason. I would find him out.

At that moment I felt the back of my neck grow light and stinging, as if cold metal had grazed it. Maybe Dennis was sitting at his desk, watching me at this very moment, tapping a pencil against his teeth while he waited for a sentence to jell. Or maybe I felt my own guilt at this fantastic disloyalty. Just then the dogs discovered me. I reduced them to wriggling ecstasy with petting, so grateful was I for their innocent and uncritical enthusiasm, their foolish burrowing noses. I raced them back to the house without looking up at the window.

By dinner time I was subdued, wondering only what grievance I'd tucked up my sleeve to cause such ill-humor, or which of my glands had gone pale and lazy. Dennis took his place at the table and I asked, as I always did, How did it go?

Inevitably he answered something laconic, like Not bad or Who knows or, more simply, Terrible. But tonight he looked at me with sour impatience, his mouth going heavy. I wish you'd stop asking me that, he said. All it does is put me on the spot.

I retreated into wounded politeness. Sorry. Didn't mean it.

It's just that I don't always feel like talking about it.

You never feel like talking about it, I said, keeping my voice mild though I felt my earlier scorn stir within me. You might as well work for the CIA.

He shrugged. Might as well.

Silence as we ladled stew onto our plates. While we're on it, said Dennis, there's something I'd appreciate. Please don't go out back while I'm working. I find it very distracting.

I stared at him but he was examining his silverware as if it were novel and intricate machinery. Very well, I said after a moment.

The second time I saw the boy was a blue April morning, the ground powdery and hot underfoot, the wind fallen to a breath, everything, it seemed, on the verge of motion. I was not thinking of him even though I sat in a forked root of the sweet gum where I'd seen him before. I was dropping stones into the creek below, enjoying their solid chunking sound, the ruffled stream. I think I could have sat there for hours, emptying my mind of everything but rock and water.

This time he did not startle me, for I saw him some distance away. Again he was fishing, wading a hundred yards away where the creek ran between two sunny pastures. I thought it odd that anyone would fish here, especially fly casting. Surely the creek was too small to support any sizable fish. I watched his arm go back, hesitate, then cast, a jerky over-strenuous movement, as if he were throwing the arm itself. He's practicing, I thought. A country kid with nowhere better to go, pretending he's in a mountain torrent. I watched, amused.

He was working his way toward me, downstream. Because of where I sat he would not see until he was quite close. The rolled edges of his jeans were dark and sopping. He bent to scoop something from the surface of the water. The line of his body from shoulder to hip to knee was spare, light, the muscles lean and just developing. It was like watching a solemn young animal try its new strength. I felt wistful, almost nostalgic, though I knew I had never been so clean-limbed and unself-conscious when I was his age.

The boy was close enough now for me to see his long, serious face, black eyebrows meshed in concentration, his cheek pouching where his tongue jutted. He was a nice-looking boy, I thought, or would be once he outgrew his adolescent rawness. His dark hair fell just below his ears, straight as cloth. Where the hot sunlight touched it was a rim of reddish gold.

Not until he was almost level with the tree did he see me. With his arm back, ready to cast, his eyes grew and wavered. The cast was wilder than usual, landing with a flat smack.

I nodded to him and, in a process that was nearly visible, he debated whether or not to acknowledge me. Finally he settled for a tilt of the head and moved past me, all constraint. I stood, dusted off my gritty legs and walked home.

That night Dennis and I sat watching a video drama intended to simulate life as we know it. Does anyone, I said, peering at the screen, have teeth like that?

Dennis kept his eyes on the television, even though now it was attempting, at top volume, to persuade us we needed an electric corn popper. I waited for him to acknowledge my remark, waited, then sank back into my chair. He had been doing some long-neglected schoolwork. The papers, looking rather soiled, lay at his feet. Thirty earnest/sloppy/tortured comparisons of Emerson and Thoreau. For the moment, they were mute.

Finally, as the drama resumed, Dennis said It's not just the way they look. It's the exaggeration, the overacting. Everything has to be visible. He nodded, as if convinced by his own argument.

I agreed with him. Right out front and larger than life.

Look at that. He indicated a woman whose clenched fists and heaving bosom represented Anger as clearly as a medieval allegory. You've betrayed me, she was saying through the obligatory clenched teeth. What a fool I've been, a blind fool, not to notice you and Sheila— Here the well-modulated voice of her male counterpart broke in. Laura, I swear, we never meant to hurt you—

Ugh, said Dennis. In the first place, nobody goes around confessing their affairs.

Well, not in such grandiose language, that's the whole point.

He shook his head, smiling down at the huddled papers as if they secretly amused him. The cowlick was working itself loose from the morning's combing. A tassle of mussed straw. People don't confess unless they think they'll be caught anyway. It's just not human nature.

Oh come on, Dennis. Surely you don't believe that.

Well, if you were having an affair I wouldn't expect to hear about it.

He was still smiling, his voice reasonable, the little tuft of hair giving him an impish look.

You wouldn't expect to, or you wouldn't want to?

Both. Would you want to hear about my affairs?

Well no, I said. But he was confusing the issue. It wasn't just that I didn't want to hear about his affairs; I didn't want him to have any. I would have told him that but he still wore his secret ironic smile and I couldn't decide which annoyed me more, his smiling or his cowlick.

Meanwhile the TV show had resolved itself through a series of unlikely events: chase scenes, sudden deaths, coincidence, catharsis. Dennis yawned and his finger hovered over the controls. Want to watch any more? I shook my head and he punched it off.

I got into bed first and watched him as he moved around the room, flipping socks and wadded underwear into corners. The single downturned beam of the Tensor lamp sculpted the walls into fans of light, huge looping shadows. Dennis sat on the edge of the bed and his backbone was transformed into exaggerated ridges and hollows, as dramatic as a dinosaur skeleton or the girders of a bridge.

Dennis, I said, speaking to that fantastic structure, do you use real people when you write?

He turned and his face was thrown into the same strange relief. His eyes and nose dripped shadows, like an exotic mask. It's all fiction, you know that. You draw on every bit of experience but nothing is a literal model. What brought that on?

Just curious. He reached for the alarm clock, set it. Do you write about me? I persisted.

He clicked the lamp off and slid under the covers before he answered. Of course not. I just explained it to you.

I see.

I lay on my side, facing him while he settled himself. I knew we would not make love tonight, knew it as clearly as if we had announced it. With my eyes open in the dark I kissed him and lay back, waiting for sleep.

The next day, the thirty-eighth, the sky was overcast, monotone, as if it were made of pale gray rubber. Around noon it began to rain. I could hear the slow trickling as the gutters emptied into the cistern. Rain at last. The patch of bare dirt by the front door was so hardened it repelled the first drops, sent them skipping up again for an instant.

By 1:00 it had stopped. The TV weatherman would call it too little too late. I felt listless, unable to concentrate on the laundry or letter writing. I went upstairs and lay down, though I knew I wouldn't sleep.

My eyes drifted across the scabby plaster of the ceiling. I thought of trying to see things in the pattern of damp spots and cracks, but I was never very good at that game. I wouldn't stay distracted. Inevitably my imagination produced faces, ships, landscapes, then thoughts of a new paint job, then led back through some subterranean route to whatever it was I had been worrying about in the first place. It depressed me to have such an unruly mind. Then I felt a small, familiar, tearing pain in my belly and rolled over, massaging it.

So that was it. The glumness, the fatigue were premenstrual, totally explainable. It would be an irony if indeed it came on this day of dribbling rain. But no, it would hold off.

Besides, I was never late, never anxious, never had to calculate my days. Compared with the weather, I was a certain forecast. It was very convenient, but sometimes I felt a little guilty. As if there were something unnatural about rejoicing in my punctual barrenness. I thought of the smooth rosy walls of my uterus, rejecting sperm and egg with calm obedience, as if they had read all the birth control pamphlets and agreed with them. How many witches had been burned for blighting conception? What they were accused of doing with knotted strings and dung, we now accomplished routinely with chemicals and copper wire.

Of course we were not trying to have children. We wanted them in some undefined future, but not now. In what unremembered past had we agreed to this? The scenes of our meeting, our marriage slurred together in my mind as I tried to isolate the one I needed. I recalled our wedding, the heap of glads and carnations on the altar, motionless in the weak November light, Dennis worrying afterwards that we'd miss our plane. No, it had not been part of the ceremony, the contract . . .

I simply couldn't remember when we'd discussed it. Perhaps we never had, it was just assumed we'd wait, it was good manners, good planning. Nothing to interrupt our calm routines of leisure and work. But the leisure was mine, a trifle, an insignificance; the work was his, oh yes, his work again!

I got up, telling myself there was no point in brooding like this. I'd purge my ill-humor with a load of laundry, fill the air with the smell of bleach and soapy water. But on the landing I hesitated, and instead of going downstairs I entered Dennis's study. My muscles cramped sharply in their blind cycle, and I kneaded them with my fist.

It was odd, how seldom I was in this room. I might empty the ashtrays or bring Dennis his coffee in the evenings, but these were brisk, distracted visits. Now the silence seemed mysterious, Dennis's presence made even more distinct by his absence, as an empty church still echoes with prayers.

And what was this holy of holies. A floor of bare gnarled boards, a battered desk and chair. The original wallpaper, he said, was good enough for him: rococo, Cinderella-style coaches, dark green, rolling in a maddening repetitive line. I observed the glass of the windows—smeared—gazed at the books on his shelves. It was like being in one of those historic houses protected by velvet ropes. But why, I thought, suddenly angry, should I feel like an intruder, what was I not allowed to share and why? I yanked open the drawers of the desk, reckless of whether or not I was disturbing anything. Envelopes, stacks of crisp blank paper, old key chains, matches, string, stamps, nothing but the expected. I tugged at the last drawer. It was locked.

I rushed down the stairs, almost falling, I lurched against the dining room table, digging a corner into my hip. I screamed, my lungs shuddering, the next intake of breath convulsive, raw, and as I stood there, not knowing whether I would scream again or once more distract my belly's pain with that sharp corner, I heard the driveway gravel crumble beneath the car's wheels.

I didn't move until the back door opened. Then I slipped into the bathroom and turned the faucet on full blast, as if the violence in me were audible, needed to be drowned out. My face in the mirror was patched with red and white, glazed, dumb, furious, my hair wild. I heard Dennis call Hello, and I answered Hello, the word coming out lilting, natural, though my mouth seemed about to spit. I buried my face in the cold water but it stung. I smoothed my hair and opened the door.

He was on the couch, flipping through *Newsweek*. He glanced up, smiling. Hiya.

Hi. I stood, leaning against the door, wondering if I looked normal again, or was it just that he never noticed anything?

After a minute he spoke again. Ready for lunch?

I'm not hungry. I had a late breakfast.

He shrugged. I'll find something for myself then.

The pages of the magazine fluttered. He was reading about new hope for cancer patients, about Broadway shows and endangered whales. I said And then you're going to work.

He looked at me. Maybe my voice had some tinge of irony or threat, but all he said was That's right.

I walked to the window, strained to see the horizon, but it was dim with wind-borne dust the rain had not settled. I wonder, I said, what your book will turn out to be. I bet you're writing—let's see—a fantasy. Life in the year 3000, that sort of thing.

In the glass of the window I saw his face reflected, half-cautious, half-amused. Nope, that's not it.

No? I turned, feeling in control now, able to shape my lips into a smile. Then it must be, you know, like *Rosemary's Baby.* A thriller.

He shook his head. Where do you get these ideas?

Oh I don't know. Is it one of those autobiographical things, portrait of the artist as an Ohio adolescent? Where you have to figure out if the towns are real places?

Honestly, said Dennis. You don't give me much credit.

He dropped his eyes to the magazine and for just a moment a pink warmth rose from his collar, the veins standing out like wires or fingers, just a moment but enough to tell me I was right. And I knew he had some part of me in that locked drawer, like a voodoo priest's hunk of rags and hair. Somewhere in those pages was my image, words shaped by his vanity, his evasiveness. What did he know of me anyway, what did he ever know? Didn't he always prefer distance to closeness, sentiment to love? At that instant I felt the blood slipping from my loins and I was fiercely glad of my emptiness for I wanted no child, no part of him, in fact I hated him.

What I said was: I'm not even close, huh?

Nope, Dennis said, folding his magazine, yawning, padding to the kitchen to fix his sandwich.

It was not that I changed my mind. In the next few days my feeling grew, or rather, I came to know the shape of it, like a smooth stone kept in a pocket and fingered constantly. The sight of his wet skull after a shower made me shiver with disgust. His square dull teeth displayed in a smile, his speech, his silence, his small pretensions, all this was now intolerable. At night I lay with each muscle clenched. If he had touched me, I think I would have struck him.

Perhaps he hesitated in the dark and decided it wasn't worth the effort.

But to put things into words and reasons? The surface of our lives left no place to drive such a wedge. Our little talk of coffee and the late show. How hard it was to shatter. And I despised him even more, realizing that this was how he wanted things.

I couldn't simply pack and leave, not without speaking. No, I had my secret words just as he did, and I was determined to say them. If only I could paint each room with blood! Then when he came home as usual, then he might ask Is anything wrong?

Eventually I would blurt something out, something hoarse and incoherent that would make him look puzzled and ask me to repeat it, was I sure I meant this instead of that? He would give me a dozen reasons why I did not feel the way I thought I did and I would sob, messy and still defeated. Eventually the sky would split and the earth turn black in a soaking rain, the new leaves shredding in cold wind, rocks boiling up from the mud as a hillside sank away. Nothing would stay as it was, but for once I wished to shape things as I chose.

It was Saturday, the house still smelling heavily of bacon. Dennis spent the morning reading term papers on the couch, wrapped in his old plaid bathrobe with one sleeve hanging by threads. Whenever he turned a page the skin gaped, pink and somehow startling, like the cheeks of an ass.

I sat at the window filing my nails. I said You should get a new bathrobe.

Mm. Can't we fix this one?

No. I sawed at my index finger. The nail snapped. I would have to cut them all short. Dennis read with his chin sunk on his chest. I could tell him it caused wrinkles in the neck, if I wanted to.

I stood. Think I'll go for a walk.

The paper slid to the floor and he picked up the next one.

Outside, the fierce sun made my scalp tighten. A glaring, summery heat covered everything like a layer of glass. When I looked into the sky, black churning spots floated across my vision. The dogs lay panting on the cool cement of the porch, but they

scrambled to follow me. The pointer smelled something at the edge
of the road, rabbit probably, and both of them went bounding into a
field. If they caught it they would spend the night coughing up
hunks of sour fur.

I was thinking of the dead boy again, for I noticed that his tree
was beginning to leaf. It was beautiful in its new airy greenness. The
death at its roots had not made it grow into some terrible distorted
shape. Nothing could be more natural than that death, the tree
seemed to say, nothing more natural than the killing force of love. It
was imagination which gave the bare facts labels: pathetic, grim,
tragic, like trying on so many hats, robbing events of their simple
truth.

I felt headachy, weak, the heat pressing on me. I told myself not
to think such things, too much thinking made you ill, mad, it should
be guarded against. I kicked off my sandals, skidded down the slope
and plunged into the water up to mid-thigh, but its force and cold-
ness made me stagger. The footing underneath was soft sucking
mud; I tried to kick myself loose from it. I wallowed and splashed
for the bank, less than a yard away, wanting only to free myself from
that unseen slime. Then, suddenly, the boy was squatting on the
creek's edge, holding out his hand to me. Here, he was saying, Here.
Perhaps he had been there all along.

I grasped his hand, it felt hot and rough and I held it only long
enough to get my balance. Thank you, I murmured, keeping my
eyes down, for I hated to think what I had looked like thrashing
around in there. I pulled myself onto the bank and, still without
looking at him, explained. It's not that I was afraid of falling, just
that the bottom feels so nasty.

Yeah, he said, but it was noncommittal. He was still crouched
with his arms folded across his legs, gazing up into the branches of
the sweet gum. No doubt he thought I was a fool, a crazy woman
leaping into a creek and then too clumsy to get herself out. His disdain was palpable, and I longed to crack his male aloofness, unsettle
it.

I turned to the boy, trying to force his eyes to mine. He didn't look
at me but he felt my gaze. He brushed his dark hair behind his ear

and a few damp strands clung to his high forehead. The attempt to seem nonchalant made him look even younger.

You fish here, don't you?

He searched the leaves again. Yeah.

Ever catch anything?

Sure. All the time.

I could tell he was lying, or at least exaggerating. At any moment he would rise, mutter some excuse, and leave. I spoke quickly. Let's see, I bet you're . . . seventeen, no, sixteen.

His skin was still smooth, the down on it just beginning to toast. Now he reddened, answered without looking at me. Sixteen.

Sixteen, I repeated, my tone marveling. Old enough to drive but not to drink. Old enough to want a girl but not to have one. He swiveled on his heels, his eyes narrowing with alarm and suspicion. Now I could see his urge for flight battling with fascination, like someone at the scene of a car accident.

Do you have a girl, I asked, not waiting for an answer. I bet you wouldn't know what to say to her anyway.

He seemed immobilized, his mouth sagging open. Yes, I thought, he would get girls, there would be no stopping it, the old misery of colliding souls. It would be better for the whole race to disappear rather than keep breeding unhappiness.

He didn't speak, just shifted his feet in the dirt. I could see his eyes looking up secretly from beneath his lashes. And I knew he wouldn't understand or believe anything I said, he would only store it up to tell some other smirking kid. Very well. We'd see about that. Just imagine, I said, keeping my voice calm, you're with your first girl. You've wrestled her underwear off in some back seat, that's how it usually goes. And you're trying not to think of anything, because the more you think the harder it'll be. In a way, see, all you want is for it to be over. But I want you to remember what I'm going to say. I want you to look at that girl and wonder what's going through her mind.

I spoke slowly, searching for words that would follow him, lie buried in the folds of the brain. Because you'll never know, will you? Maybe she's thinking about love, that would be nice. But maybe she's pretending you're somebody else. You don't know. Or maybe she's not really part of what's happening at all, she's disgusted with all the grunting and sweating and grappling, she's thinking you're ridiculous, a clown—

He was on his feet by now, striding away. A clown, I called after him. Don't you forget it.

I sat for a minute longer, feeling the heat of the day sift through the leaves, feeling it wrap my bare legs until the skin felt taut and parched. I reached for my sandals. I whistled for the dogs but they were far away by now.

When I walked in the house Dennis was still lying on the couch. He glanced up and smiled at me. I stood before him. My eyes retained the round hot circle of the sun as if holes were cut in my retinas, flickering black, then orange. I have something to tell you, I said.

Bess the Landlord's Daughter

I like to think I'm cynical about all the right things. By that I mean anything that tries to convince everyone, unanimously and indiscriminately, like politics or advertising, or slick mass-produced romance. I'm talking about the languishing goop you hear on the radio or the publicity for certain over-popular movies. The broken hearts are as large as billboards, roaring and baying at you. The framed engravings that hung in the Westicott Hotel were simply an older version of the same tradition.

These were pale cheaply printed things from the turn of the century and the one I remember best had faded so badly its title was quite gone. It was probably something like The Warrior's Farewell or Loved I Not Honor More. A natty young soldier in splendid uniform embraces his beloved. There is something a little askew about his posture, suggesting that he is either in the grip of passion or restraining his impatience to be gone. The maiden, curiously, is not looking at him but at us. She is pale, plump, even rather seal-shaped. It is the convention of the scene, not her expression, that tells us she is suffering. She looks glum but stolid. The artist has furnished her with a terrier, who looks puzzled.

Such stuff begs for satire. It comes easily and we're proud to have proven ourselves so discerning and cynical. Cynicism, after all, is the coin of the realm these days. But when it comes to a real-life sentimental possibility I can't always muster that reflex snigger. You might say I climb inside the frame with the soldier and his drooping lady. So I regarded that first encounter between Bess and Stephen. I imagined how he must have seemed to her with his good manners and soft eyes and voice and when I thought of it as charming it did not occur to me that this was romanticism.

What really happened, what I know for sure, is that Stephen came back to the car with the room key and said It's even better inside and only fifteen a night. I'm willing to risk the plumbing if you are. I said God yes, anything to get out of this car.

So we hauled our bulging suitcases out of the trunk. I felt wrinkled and stiff and unclean. Doughnut crumbs and Kleenex adhered to my clothes. We crossed the bare porch boards of the Westicott Hotel, which creaked, and I smiled at the girl who held the door open for us.

Stephen and I had been driving all week without covering much ground, the type of vacation we preferred. The New England landscape was exotic to us and we purposely chose the most convoluted and obscure highways. We noted each gabled house, each red barn and shady pasture with satisfaction. Everyone knows the things you see along such roads. The meticulous, rather intimidating restored houses. The old graveyards and the plaques which tell you about church sites and massacres. The profusion of shops selling antiques and syrup and crafts and cheese, all of them named as coyly as possible, the Calico this, the Cozy that, the Red Pony, the Blue Mill. The ruins of less successful shops falling into decay like a layer of mulch. We admired everything. The same sort of taste, and an overheating engine, led us to the Westicott.

We were entering one of the more solemnly historic towns. There was a grove of those severely maintained, barn-sized Colonial houses, all painted white, there were the usual church and monument. It was mid-summer and the well-tended grass was emerald, the shade trees heavy. Pink and lavender impatiens grew in pots on the doorsteps. Stephen and I were clucking in a helpless inarticulate fashion when we rounded a corner and exclaimed.

Such a ruin, I said, before we noticed the curtains in the windows. Then I saw the sign.

Stephen was not as immediately enthusiastic as I was. He'd been driving for the last three hours and was not in a mood to experiment with his comfort. A place like that could mildew your clothes overnight, was what he said. But I knew I could convince him, so I just said Let's drive around town and see what else there is. We looked at the standard sanitized pool, A/C, C/TV, phones places, the like of which we'd been staying in for so long, and turned back.

It was surely romantic to choose such a place. I waited in the car for Stephen, feeling pleased with myself. The Westicott was hideous and irresistible. Even in that neighborhood of enormous structures it was a monster, five levels high at some points, not counting the cellar. Two sagging wings were attached to the main block of the house. There was not a flake of paint left on any outside surface, which gave it the look of having rusted, or perhaps of having already burned down. I never found out if the Westicotts were exempted from the seemingly obligatory spiffiness of the rest of town, or if they refused to paint, or simply couldn't afford it. The last seems most likely. A verandah edged two sides of the house and this was lined with wicker rockers and huge potted ferns. The shade trees had nearly swallowed the first floor. White ruffled curtains hung at the windows. Around back, a bushel basket with the bottom punched out had been nailed to the wall for a basketball hoop.

I didn't take much notice of Bess the first time I saw her. I call her Bess, although her real name was something more like Audrey or Joann, because she deserved a better, more fragrant name. And she made me think of "The Highwayman," which I had to memorize in seventh grade and still carry around scraps of:

> Bess the landlord's daughter
> The landlord's black-eyed daughter
> Plaiting the dark red love-knot
> Into her long black hair

Of course it was an ironic association, one I concocted to amuse myself. This Bess was a short silent girl of fifteen or so, dark-eyed, to be sure, but bespectacled, her brown hair cut straight and chinlength. Her face was round and rather soft and she was probably more pretty than plain, or so you would have said if she had been the sort of girl anyone looked at more than once. She wore jeans and flannel shirts and it was pure whimsey for me to associate her with the love, betrayal, and passion of the ballad.

All this came later. My only impression, when I smiled at her at the door of the Westicott, was of a tremendous, studious reserve. If she could have been treated as part of the furniture it would have been a relief to her. As it was, when I smiled she flinched as if I had gnashed my teeth. Later I thought it was because of Stephen. Still later I wondered what I had looked like padding up those stairs. Bare-foot, wild-haired, grinning hugely—I might have been expected to startle her.

We dropped our suitcases and stretched out on the bed, enjoying our exhaustion. Stephen sighed and I massaged his neck. We are happiest like this, curled together like a pair of old dogs, and we might have fallen asleep right then if Stephen hadn't remembered the car.

He hoisted himself up and said I guess I'd better find a garage before it gets any later. His tone was gloomy since he knew I would not contradict him. I watched him assemble his shoes and keys and bill-fold, thinking how attractive he looked, even this tired and wrinkled, and how unaware of it he was. Stephen appeals to women because he is this quiet and unassuming and makes them feel that no one else has ever noticed his particular beauty before. Admiring him gives you the impression of discovery.

I sat up also. Do you want me to go with you?

He said, as I knew he would, No, stay here and relax. It won't take long. But I expect we'll have to leave it overnight.

Oh well, I said, sounding the first note of resigned acceptance. If one of us begins it, the other will usually pick it up. Mustn't grumble, can't be helped, and so on.

He smiled and leaned over to smooth my hair. Maybe you can take a nap before dinner.

Although I agreed to this and got under the covers, as soon as he left I knew I wouldn't sleep. Instead I got up and prowled the room. It was twice as large as the standard motel offering and smelled wonderfully of what I guessed was lavender. The fireplace, for there was a fireplace, was marble, a coal burner, with a big carved-frame mirror above it. Although we were to learn that the house dated from 1790, the impression it gave was Early Victorian, clean but rather worn. The three good pieces of furniture bore this out. The bed and two marble-topped dressers were ornamented, but in a blocky fashion, tending toward square corners and simple carved bosses. There were overlapping carpets, all nearly colorless, and new yellow wallpaper.

The bathroom, really, was no worse than you'd expect.

I opened our door with caution, for it was the kind of echoing portentous place that made you move stealthily. As far as I could tell there was no one but ourselves staying there. A long corridor contained other guest rooms, none quite as nice as ours but all furnished in the same whimsical and threadbare fashion. Three staircases led up to the different wings. Through a dim glass panel in a door marked Dining Room I saw ranks of tables, each linen covered and each with its four chairs still set about it, though the hotel had obviously not served meals in years. This struck me as rather ghostly and horrible, as if invisible meals might be left there at night for spirits. Turning, I almost ran into Bess.

She had a real facility for moving quietly through those dim hallways. How long she had been there watching me I don't know. I started and stammered a bit, then laughed.

This is a spooky place, I said. Then I thought that might be taken as an insult so I added That's part of the fun, isn't it?

Of course it was her expression which made me think I'd insulted her. Her lips twitched, a polite little reflex. Of the two of us she was by far the more self-possessed. I began to think she was not so much shy as she was wearily inured to endless strangers in her home, though not inured enough to be anything but resentful of them. I'd certainly felt that way at her age: People were stupid, intolerable, would they never leave you alone? She was about to pass when I said Could I get some drinking water from you? Here, like most places in the area, the tap water was contaminated.

She turned, opened the door to the cellar, and flicked a light switch. Standing where I was, only a little to one side, I still couldn't see anything but darkness. That unnerved me. Bess returned, pressed the phantom light switch, and handed me a thick glass pitcher full of yellow-tinted water.

Thank you, I said, then, wanting to hold her a little longer (I was already curious about her as well as the house) I asked if anyone would mind if I looked around a bit. It's such a marvelous house. Her silence seemed to provoke me into heaping one inanity on another. You're so lucky to live here, I told her.

She dropped her eyes, as if the glasses, the fringe of bangs, the weak light of the hall still failed to shield her adequately. She made a noise of cautious assent.

Could I see the upstairs?

Those are family rooms, she stated, her voice, although mild, containing no hint of human warmth, only of wariness. In this she was very much like her mother. I apologized and retreated.

Bess's family contributed largely to the picture I formed of her. Of course you could draw certain conclusions from her own behavior, such as her habit of sitting, neither reading nor conversing, for an hour at a time, on the porch, the stairs, or in the semi-public parlor on the first floor. She sat with a kind of determined passivity that was the very opposite of restlessness, like old people often sit. Her grandmother, in fact, had the same posture though she managed to look more contented.

This was the family: Bess, her mother, and grandmother. Whatever men they'd had were lost, stolen or strayed, dead, deserted, absent. More than most houses, the Westicott could have used a handyman. The family resemblance among the three women was so striking as to be acutely depressing. There was Bess, still fresh and not uncomely, and the dumpy stern unfashionable mother, and the vague grandmother. All wore spectacles. With each generation the face grew a little more undefined, the chin looser. I'm sure they were aware of it themselves. At least the grandmother had achieved good humor. It was she who answered our questions about the house, as best she could through her deafness, while Bess sat nearby, murmuring occasional corrections.

Perhaps, no doubt, Bess had friends her own age, normal teenage intrigues and interests. So I tell myself. Once the phone rang, and her mother came out to the porch and summoned Bess. Through an open window I saw her sitting with the phone clamped painfully between her chin and shoulder. She said No. No, not really. Then she said, with more emphasis, It doesn't make any difference to me. When she returned to the porch her expression was just as dead as before.

It is entirely possible that our brief visit gave me a false impression of her isolation. But I must disclaim my disclaimers and say that her situation seemed quite paralyzed to me, quite unhappy. There was that emanation of exclusion and disapproval from those other well-groomed houses. There was the certainty that she would inherit the crumbling hotel, losing one room at a time to damp rot and winter storms. Already the top two and a half floors were uninhabited, peeling away to reveal sky. In the last rooms she would grow chins among the weeping ferns and white curtains.

When Stephen came back and said the car could not even be promised for tomorrow, I was annoyed, then resigned. We walked into the village for a good dinner and to see the sights, which were mostly tombstones. On our way back we dawdled. The Westicott, wrapped in its heavy maples, seemed to be settling unevenly into the ground. The few lights near the front only made the black bulk of it seem sterner.

It looks like a mouthful of broken teeth, said Stephen, halting on the corner.

Or the haunted house from Disneyland. Oh hell, why did I have to say that.

Stephen was amused. Why not?

Because now I'll think about haunted houses and convince myself they really do exist, you know, in the newest psuedo-scientific fashion—people leave electrical impulses behind them, or soul-energy, or something. And the blobs of energy will come mess up my electrons for making fun of them.

Well if you can talk about it like that you surely can't be too superstitious.

It's not superstition, I just know how I'll feel. The same thing happens if I go to a fortune teller. I get really *sweaty,* even though all they ever say is they see the state of Florida and the number seven.

You just enjoy scaring yourself. No, you enjoy trying to scare yourself but it's never genuine, said Stephen, which I denied, and on which he insisted, the conversation degenerating, or maybe progressing, into sexual teasing. Just before the hotel we kissed and continued walking hand in hand.

Not until we reached the porch did we realize that Bess and her grandmother were stationed there. I suppose if we'd tried to stage a demonstration of a charming, affectionate young couple we couldn't have been more successful. The rocking chairs made the faintest dry whirring sound, like an insect closed up in an empty room. The old lady called out to us and asked us if we'd had a pleasant evening. We stood in front of them. The streetlight tinted the four moons of their glasses.

A very pleasant evening, we both replied. A lovely town.

Such fine weather, she insisted, imagining that we must have mentioned that also. Good for sleeping, on the cool side. There were blankets in the room if we needed them.

Oh, we won't have any trouble keeping warm, I said, and in the dark Stephen nudged my ribs. Of course the old lady noticed nothing and Bess, who noticed everything, said nothing. Well goodnight now, I said, trying to keep the giggle out of my voice. We passed inside and one of the rockers creaked.

I didn't sleep well that night. The antique bedstead was built for a narrower generation. The boards at the head and foot gave me the impression of being inside a shoebox and every time I drifted off to sleep I'd wake up deeply embedded in the soft mattress. Whenever this happened I'd be fully and hopelessly awake. The big house was silent. I was looking up at the pale bar of light on the ceiling, the seepage of hall lamp from under the door, when suddenly it was obliterated.

I couldn't move. Then a knife-edge of light reappeared. I can't judge how long it took me to raise myself, muscle by muscle, taking great care not to make the springs creak. What I saw was the double smudge of feet blocking the line of light. Beside me Stephen breathed heavily in sleep. I can scream, I thought, I can wake him up. What happened was that after another moment the shadow removed itself. Again there was no sound anywhere.

The next day I decided it had been Bess, both from the lack of other plausible suspects and from another incident. The way it came about was this. We were joined that day by another lodger who Stephen and I named the Jolly One. He was a young man, though his weight made him seem older and more imposing, traveling alone from Kansas to Boston. Just for the hell of it, he said, obviously proud of his impulsiveness. The Jolly One loved everything about the hotel and the town and I suppose his enthusiasm was really no sillier than our own. But the Jolly One had a perfectly spontaneous unreserve that allowed him to speak of his plans and admirations to anyone he had just encountered. We first became aware of him at lunch time when, rounding the corner of the house, we saw a majestic dimpled rump bent over the front seat of a car. When he heard us he straightened, laughed, and, not at all embarrassed, said Hi, here's the other end. The Jolly One wore jeans and denim shirts, clothes that were appropriate for his age but which seemed incongruous, as if a wrestler had costumed himself as a Kansas farm boy. This place is really something, really a find, he kept repeating, nodding at the hotel with an almost proprietary air. I felt a little like Bess, shrinking from so much approval. All day we heard his high, pleasant fat man's laughter assaulting the walls. He made us realize how quiet the family upstairs had been.

It took such an exuberant personality to meld us all into any kind of social unit. That afternoon Stephen and I emerged from our room after a nap, feeling a little glazed. It's depressing to think what the lack of a television can do to you. We nodded to Bess and her mother, who had taken up their stations on the porch, and settled in a little distance away with the newspapers. So we would have stayed had not the Jolly One, in a billowing lime-green windbreaker, appeared on the sidewalk fresh from sightseeing.

He helloed us all, it was impossible not to acknowledge him, and when he began talking we each felt ourselves addressed and had to attend. Bess's grandmother emerged, drawn by a voice loud enough to pierce her deafness. The Jolly One had brown thick close-cut hair like fur, bright brown eyes, and layers of healthy pink skin. He was perfectly good-humored and he bullied us into sociability, traveling from one end of the porch to the other. Ma'am, what's the name of that house there, no, that one, and is it open to the public? It's a beauty. He wanted a picture of it. Had Stephen taken many pictures? He'd gotten some dandies. Maybe I wouldn't mind if he took my picture right where I sat, just like that?

In this way he gave a temporary unity to the group on the porch, and from the questions he asked Bess's grandmother we learned more about the hotel. Stages traveling between Boston and Montreal had stopped here. Their family had owned it for almost a hundred years. They built them to last back then. The Jolly One had even succeeded in directing questions to Bess. It was strange for me to hear her speak, for I had begun to think of her as a gloomy presence rather than a fellow creature who could answer questions civilly. Yes, she helped out quite a bit with the hotel but as it was only open spring through fall it didn't interfere with her schoolwork. She was studying French. She didn't mind the winters, you could ski then. He succeeded in drawing out a perfect stream of mundane information, though not once did she volunteer a remark of her own.

It was while the Jolly One was telling us of some adventure that I happened to glance at Bess. A pillar hid her from everyone's view but mine when I leaned back far enough. She was looking at Stephen. For a moment I was startled, but only for a moment, because then everything made perfect sense to me. It was only too predictable that she should look at him this way, she who must regard the parade of guests as endless possibilities and constant disappointments. There could be no highwaymen or redcoats here, only people who complained about the drafts and left a mound of dirty linen behind them. Still, she could look. At her age sometimes you only had to look at a man to have all of him that you needed. He would be a half-imagined figure she could summon until the next figure came along, just as the enormous faces on movie screens shrink obligingly for private fantasies. So she watched Stephen, quite without her usual furtiveness, not bothering to shield herself with her hair or hands or posture. Her expression was not yearning or moony but steadily intent and greedy for as long as the Jolly One's story lasted.

Shortly after that Bess's mother and grandmother went upstairs and I made some excuse to go to the room. I now recalled other moments, fragments, things I had seen but not suspected at the time. I was glad I hadn't said anything about last night to Stephen. It did not trouble me at all that Bess had stood outside our door to listen to his breathing. If I could help to leave them alone together it might make her happy, at least in the way that fifteen can be happy.

It was half an hour or so later that Stephen came in and lay down on the bed. The Jolly One even loves climbing hills, he announced. You can't do that very much back in Kansas.

Have you been talking to him all this time?

No, thank God. He took off to see the third oldest church or the fourth most decisive battlefield or something.

Stephen buried his face in the pillows. I tugged at his hair. And did the little girl say anything, I asked him at last.

She and the Jolly One discussed the fall foliage.

I thought, yes, that was how one went about it, you displayed yourself casually, as if all your interest was in the fall foliage, careless of your real object. When you were left alone you fell silent. Stephen had no doubt read his newspaper the whole time. I lay down beside him, perfectly content, and coaxed us into lovemaking.

That night we were visited again. I must have heard something this time because I woke quite suddenly, knowing we were not alone. Again the ceiling darkened. If I could have spoken to her I would have said By tomorrow we'll be gone. These feelings are treacherous and uncontrollable, other people have lived through them and if it is any consolation, you will too. But what you need, what you really ought to do, is turn this house into the funeral home it so much resembles and find yourself a good solid awkward boy who'll take you to live in an apartment complex like the rest of the world does.

Imagine giving anyone such advice, imagine anyone accepting it. But I did clear my throat, very deliberately and wakefully, out of some wish to tell her I knew or perhaps as a warning. The light on the ceiling blinked again; she had gone.

In the morning Stephen went to ransom the car while I settled our

bill at the hotel. I gave the key to Bess's mother, who forgot herself
enough to smile. She sat behind a high oak counter, banked by
pigeonholes and a glass-doored cabinet displaying sea shells. I took
a last look at this room, which managed to please and depress me in
equal measures. It combined the stately furniture of some long-dead
ancestor with the haphazard clutter of the living and the reminders
of vanished prosperity. The brown leather ledger in which you reg-
istered was charming, as was the old tin match dispenser. The
bouquet of plastic lilacs and the brochures for the tourist attractions
of thirty years ago were only sad.

When I went back to fetch our suitcases I opened the door and
found Bess there. I don't know who was the more surprised. She had
been standing in the center of the room by the unmade bed, quite
vacantly it seemed, at least until I had startled her. Her hands still
dangled at her sides but her face was stricken, blank. Nothing
human remained in it now that her carefully guarded indifference
had been destroyed.

I didn't move from the doorway. It was not my intention to corner
her but she would not pass me. How long could we stay like this? An
adult with more guile would have said I need to collect the linen, or
some such excuse, but Bess was a child sealed in her fantasy. As for
me, I could invent no casual, surface remark; I remained in the
shadowy unsaid current of what had passed between us.

At last her face began to change. Blood pulsed in her throat.
From the angle where I stood I could see both the shallow mirroring
of her glasses and the tears in her eyes. It was a hopeless humilia-
tion, nothing now could erase it, but I only meant to be kind when I
said Please don't be upset. It doesn't matter, it's all right.

Bess's head slumped a little, as if she were looking for some last
hope of concealment, then she jerked it upright. Oh leave me alone!
she cried. You think you know everything! You make me sick!

I must have half-known what was coming, because I was not as
surprised at this as I might have been. She continued, still not
daring to look straight at me: I don't want your stupid sympathy,
you don't know anything at all about it!

She was both furious and mortified now, as if she had been
goaded into something against her very nature. I said, coldly, I know

you've been prowling around after my husband. I'm not that stupid.

Oh, said Bess, switching her tone to match my scorn, go ahead, make everything sound cheap and hateful, that's all you do. Everything's there for your amusement. Always prying and snooping, making your little jokes.

She was not fighting as women often do, obliquely, sneeringly, speaking of everything but the real issue. As for prying and snooping, I said, I believe you're better at it.

She glared at me, helpless in the face of this surface truth, this unfairness. For even as I stood there, coldly, composedly, I was able to defend myself against everything but the meaning of her words. People like you, they pay for a room and think they own us, she cried. They laugh at us and they know we have to put up with them—here Bess began to lose her momentum, tears making her shiver. You don't know, she managed, you don't know anything—

She shook her head, her old reflex of retreating behind her hair, and pushed past me out of the room.

A few minutes later Stephen drove up with the car. I met him on the porch with the suitcases. As we pulled away the Jolly One emerged with his camera pointed at us, clicking extravagantly. I waved, thinking of all the images of ourselves that must be imprisoned in the albums of strangers.

It does not surprise me now that hate, not love, was the climax of our stay at the Westicott. That is, if Bess "loved" Stephen, she certainly felt the opposite for me in greater measure. I think she must have disliked me from the first. Not just for Stephen's sake but because, as she accused me, I chose to make her and her world a diversion, an object of curiosity. She sensed that even though she struggled to find words for it. I am a tourist of the emotions, visiting only the most well-worn spots. It is romantic, that is, a distortion, to imagine whole lives from the barest observation. Another person might say that Bess's destiny was to procure a father for her own round-faced daughters, and that this was no less likely, no more tragic than it had been for her mother and grandmother. And the Bess of the ballad, as she pressed herself against the cold lip of the musket, may not have been thinking of love at all.

Paper Covers Rock

It seemed she didn't know what she was doing. All that winter her mind was as blank and enclosed as a bubble of glass. At the time, of course, you thought the bubble was full of opinions, plans, disappointments, and so on. But those were just reflexes. Really thinking about what she was doing would have been intolerable. It was an odd way to have a love affair.

Or maybe it was the only way. You felt the drone of your blood, the heat of your skin, and nothing else, like a cat. The winter sky streamed with rain which refused to crystallize into snow. Dripping trees ambushed her and she never arrived anywhere with dry feet. Like a cat she tended scrupulously to her own comfort at the end of the day. She bought good sherry and expensive bath salts and lolled in hot water up to her neck, sometimes falling asleep there.

Sometimes her lover arrived at that point. She'd open her eyes to see him standing over her, the blurred light behind him making it difficult to read his face. She'd missed something, she thought, by not being able to see him clearly at that moment, some clue to the future. The scented water made her feel languid, drugged. Her body seemed to undulate like a ribbon beneath it, more naked than if she were surrounded by air. He'd always wait until she was wrapped in towels, her skin shrinking a little from the sudden chill, then he'd lead her by the hand into another room.

Later, still without speaking a word, they might find their fingers curling towards their palms and one of them would start the game.

The fist beating one, two, then three, forming one of the simple shapes. Rock, scissors or paper. She didn't remember playing it as a child but now it delighted her. The awful restraint of preserving the fist, the impulse of the open hand, the more precise maneuver of the fingers. He allowed her this foolishness and she gloried in his indulgence. It pleased her to be able to ask something of him, even a small thing. They tapped each other lightly for forfeits and when one tired of playing the taps turned into caresses.

Sooner or later he always had to leave. They made a tradition of being brisk and cheerful about it. Time I put some clothes on, he'd say, and the answer to that was Only if you're going outside. She watched him from the window, wishing he had something as uncomplicated as a wife. A married lover was, after all, a situation easily defined, with its own set of precedents, its own literature.

Instead there was mutable anarchy. He was not married to the woman he lived with, that she knew. It seemed to make her own status and expectations terribly unclear. As she picked her way through the sullen water in the gutters, as the wind blew wet leaves against her ankles, she imagined encountering the two of them together. Would her lover pass without acknowledging her, in the classic manner of adulterers? Would there be accusations and speeches? That all seemed incongruous, as if they should be wearing nineteenth-century costumes.

I just want to get things straight, she said once. We're crazy in bed, it's wonderful, we shouldn't expect more than that. She saw him frown and said hurriedly I can live with it. I just want to make sure we understand each other.

He stroked her cheek with one finger, which always made her skin feel as if it would ring like fine porcelain. Why do you sell yourself short, girl? Don't cheapen things.

Maybe nobody understands how to behave anymore, she said, struggling against the lulling finger. Nobody understands what they need.

You need a good man. Someone better than me.

She thought, but did not say, A lot of good men have told me that, and pressed his full hand against her face.

Once or twice she slept with other men when her lover was not around. She wasn't sure if she should feel guilty. Similarly, she felt hesitant to label her curiosity about his mistress (his *other* mistress, she reminded herself) as jealousy. She felt like a stray particle moving outside the laws of physics.

Perhaps her lover had several mistresses, she considered, and each mistress in turn had other lovers. It was like the nursery rhyme. As I was going to St. Ives, I met a man with seven wives and every wife had seven sacks and every sack had seven cats and so on. When she reached this point it seemed to her that everyone in the world must be connected by hidden, erotic currents, everyone shared the same sly secret, and she gave up trying to make sense of it.

It didn't help to remind herself she'd wanted things this way. The first time she saw him it was the burnt end of summer. She'd been driven out of her apartment by the airless heat and boredom. The sidewalks were a baked, dazzling white as she drifted past shop windows, trying to interest herself in the premature tweeds worn by slim ecstatic mannequins. At the end of the block a figure was approaching. There was no one between them and she felt her body stiffen in preparation for the inevitable awkward moment of passing. The figure changed from a dark spot edged by glare into a tall young man with black hair and beard. She wondered briefly whether to smile or not.

They were no more than a dozen yards apart when her face turned unaccountably brittle, flushed. Was it because he was staring at her? But then (how slow the heat made everything!) she was staring at him also. They passed without speaking or smiling and she continued down the white street, wondering if she had imagined that odd moment.

The very next day she saw him drinking coffee in a restaurant. She was out of his sight and could examine him at length. Under the cool lights he looked paler, the contrast between hair and skin more pronounced. He had a newspaper spread out before him and his face was absorbed, almost stern. This time she identified her agitation as sexual. Yet she felt much more deliberate, more calculating. She left without speaking to him, sure that she'd see him again.

When she did she was surprised by how simple it was. The simplest thing in the world! She had a power she'd never suspected, maybe all women did. Hi, may I join you? she'd said. It was that easy. They sat in a bar, on opposite sides of a red vinyl booth. The seat beneath her was badly sprung and contributed to her sensation that she was about to topple over. Now the light was late-afternoon, green-tinged gold sliding through the narrow windows.

She said I imagine you're used to strange women accosting you in public. And smiled.

Matter of fact, I'm not. But I could get used to it. His voice was lighter than she'd expected, but pleasant. And she liked the way he controlled his own surprise, not allowing her to unsettle him.

I'm sure most ladies are more subtle about it. Maybe they're afraid of you.

This seemed to startle him more than her intrusion had. Afraid? Good God, I'm the most inoffensive fellow I know. I'm even polite to those evangelists who knock on your door in the morning and get you out of bed. He spread his hands. Harmless, see?

Oh but you look wicked, she said recklessly, trying to keep her momentum. You look like a pirate. Somebody who opens bottles with their teeth.

He shook his head. Maybe I should start carrying a briefcase and wearing ties.

They must have spent some time talking about neutral, informational things. She learned he worked for a radio station. He enjoyed reading novels. All the while she was at the mercy of her own sense of sight: the sunburnt ridge of his collarbone disappearing beneath a shadowy fold of cloth, pointing toward the heart. The lean, anatomical beauty of his hands. And his eyes, which could not have been more startling, blue, large-pupiled, with a dark rim around the iris. Later he would tell her about a Cherokee great-grandmother.

Finally she said I wish I could tell you how attractive I find you. Will you let me show you?

He neither smiled nor looked abashed. There's someone—he began, but she interrupted.

I don't want to hear about it. Not now, at least. He nodded and they left together. After all she had not really given him much choice.

She supposed they were both nervous; she was ready to make allowances. But there was no need to. Perhaps she had already entered that blank glass bubble where sensation replaced thought. Their nakedness pleased them both. If it had not been their first time together, they might have lingered a bit beforehand. Her apartment had a window which showed nothing but sky. They watched it pass through all the exaggerations of sunset, then turn sedate blue, then a little polished moon and one star appeared. He had to go.

Don't say anything, she told him. What could we say that would make any sense? She wanted to avoid the obligatory discussion of whether or not either of them had done this sort of thing before. The truth was she hadn't, but for the moment she wanted to pretend she had. Her new daring elated her.

You're the pirate you know, not me.

An apprentice pirate. A mere cabin boy. Good-bye now.

So she had adopted violence, impulse, anarchy, at the expense of safety. Even now she could not say she was entirely sorry. But impulse did not sustain one over a matter of months. As the interminable rains began she found herself growing melancholy, wondering what she had gotten herself into. It was mortifying to cast yourself in the role of a seductress, a woman of grand, careless passions, then find yourself yearning after something more predictable. If she'd been looking for the limits of her unorthodoxy, she'd found them.

Some evenings she fixed him a meal, or hot whiskey with lemon to guard against the dampness. At such times she was especially bright and talkative, clattering dishes in the sink, fussing over sugar bowls and napkins. This was to disguise the pleasure she took in it, and also the irony of knowing that for them this was just a parody of domestic intimacy. It was on one such occasion, sitting on the rug as he ate toasted cheese, that she asked about his girlfriend.

He looked surprised, then rather grim. Oh come on, she said. You're not going to hurt my feelings. I'm not trying to scheme or plot, I'm just curious.

Still he hesitated. She had to prod him. How long have you known her?

Three years. We met at a party, she'd come with this loud-mouth fellow who hangs around the bars. Well, he wanted her to go upstairs with him. Turns out she hardly even knew the guy. And he was shit-faced drunk. Tried to get her clothes off right in the kitchen. A real charmer.

She was fascinated, apprehensive of what she'd hear next. And then?

He shrugged. Well, I told him to lay off and when he didn't I got him bloody. Then she and I got together. He finished his sandwich; it was obvious he didn't want to say more.

She was shaken, pulled in so many different directions she didn't trust herself to look at him. First, his terseness disappointed her, she wanted to picture the incident in all its intolerable detail. The thought of him fighting, of that strength she knew so well in love erupting into violence, gave her a sharp erotic ache. It was no wonder that he and the girl had become lovers. What excited and dismayed her most of all was the evidence that he was not always the mild, obliging creature he made himself out to be. She knew that some of that was mere disclaimer, a self-effacement he felt comfortable with. But the thought that parts of him were hidden, that she could not elicit them, was intolerable.

After a moment she looked up, smiled, and extended her fist towards him. He smiled also and the game began. She was intent, almost desperate in her concentration, as if by anticipating his gestures she could read the rest of his mind. Rock, the smasher, she thought of as unadorned fact, unthinking force. Scissors were contrived, a tool, a sly edge. Paper she liked, it was harmless, it only covered rather than destroyed. Holding her breath she formed paper.

He had scissors. He tapped her wrist, then kissed her and said I have to go.

She retrieved his coat and told him to be careful driving. When he was gone she began to weep, the first tears she had ever shed over him.

The tears reached their usual anticlimactic end. She felt hot-eyed and weak. Now, she told herself, is the time to think things out. That statement had a calming effect on her until she realized she couldn't just stop there.

Again she rallied herself. She supposed her choice was either to go on as they had or stop seeing him. What did she really want? She wanted what the other woman had, his legitimate presence. Then she had to retreat from that, for what was legitimate about simple cohabitation, and did she want a lover who was unfaithful?

It was hopeless. She sat on the floor, back to the wall, legs bent crookedly beneath her. The perfect silence and the glossy black of the windows told her it was very late, that motionless hour some time before dawn when the clock's hands point to zero. She conjured up her lover, imagined his weight against her taut legs, imagined his startling pallor threaded with blue milky veins. Of course they weren't really blue at all but red, a peculiar stream branching to every part of the skin. Blood, she thought, was something she could understand, its submerged, secret channeling, its frantic movement to and from the heart . . .

Her head ached. She realized she was smashing it against the wall behind her, but the realization was so gradual she did not immediately stop, but observed herself idly for a moment. Thud. Thud. Thud. A pause, and the rhythm was repeated. She simply didn't know whether to laugh or cry. Apparently it was impossible to make your head into anything but a head. The sky was still dark when she fell asleep, sagged against the baseboard.

It rained steadily through Christmas, smearing the colored lights and making the evergreens droop. In January the rain gave way to sleet. She skimmed across the treacherous pavement and when she fell she abandoned herself to gravity, landing heavily. Often she told herself she was crazy, or going crazy, and that notion served to explain everything.

When she finally met the woman he lived with, she made another attempt at understanding it all. The circumstances were entirely innocent: she entered a bar with a man she knew casually, and someone called his name. Three people sat at a corner table—her lover, a woman, and the man who knew her friend. So without the slightest manipulation on her part she found herself sitting down with them in the neutral role of a stranger, able to watch everything.

Her first glance at the woman startled her. She was, she thought, much plainer than herself, her clothes showing only the most ineffectual attempts at vanity, her light brown hair gathered at the neck. It made her face look too round, almost bland. She stored this impression and looked away, for her lover was trying to catch her eye. At first she thought he was anxious and she tried to reassure him with a glance: don't worry, I won't blow it.

But that wasn't it. Then she knew, he was wondering about the man she was with. Oh *him,* she tried to convey, silently, lifting her shoulders to indicate a shrug, he's nothing, really, nothing at all. Though why she should apologize or justify being with another man, she didn't know.

Watching her lover's distraction and abrupt gestures, she became aware of something else. He was self-conscious about being on display, he knew she was watching the two of them with ferocious curiosity and it made him nervous. Good, she thought. This mild sadism was a novelty she enjoyed.

The woman he lived with—there was no doubt it was she—was filling the ashtray in front of her with cigarette after cigarette, dangling them between her fingers with an utter lack of interest. In fact she seemed bored with everything. She looked like the sort of woman who would use her boredom and silence as a weapon, a kind of damp club. She had pale blue eyes, very pretty, her best feature. They reminded you of the pastel flowers painted on china. Once, in the middle of a conversation about politics, she tapped him on the arm and said I've got to call Dinah. Don't let me forget. He acknowledged this and turned back to the discussion with a curtness which, watching, she felt only she understood.

She was a little sorry for him. The woman was showing such deadly low vitality, it must be painful. In such a situation one wanted to present the most invulnerable front possible. She felt sorry for the woman herself, slouching in her chair, one hand rumpling her cheek, mouth slack and pouting. Surely if she knew she was being judged she'd make more of an effort. She felt a convoluted and misplaced helpfulness, imagining how she would coach the woman, tell her to comb out her hair, use more makeup, project herself. Then she realized how hysterical she herself must be, pretending to give fashion magazine advice to her rival.

Afterward she hardly remembered the conversation, perhaps because the silence occupied her whole attention, but one part of it stuck in her mind. The man she came with said I'm so tired of this town. Not to mention the weather. I wish we could all get drunk enough to pile in a car and drive to Mexico.

Why Mexico, asked the man she didn't know.

Because it's just far enough away to be impossible, I guess. My favorite fantasy cliché.

Oh but it's not impossible, she heard herself saying. She leaned on her forearms so she was inclined toward the center of the table. We could surely get as far as Arkansas before we sobered up. We'd drive all night and by 7:00 in the morning we'd be scroungy and god-awful hung over and pissed off at each other. When was the last time you let yourself do something thoroughly stupid? It's the only way you can recapture your youth.

The others laughed, except of course the woman, who only lifted one corner of her mouth. The smile disappeared into the crease of her palm. *Screw her,* she thought, and continued, encouraged by the laughter and her own image glowing in the dim table top. We'd have breakfast in some terrible fake franchise restaurant, you know, the Farmer's Daughter or something, where the waitresses all wear pinafores, and half of us would decide to go back on the bus.

And the other half? It was her lover, and his voice managed to sound both wistful and ironic.

We'll buy a gallon of foul red wine and pledge eternal friendship and start driving again. And when we get to the border—her hands moved in a wide circle to indicate the multitude of possibilities. The guards at the border will make us paranoid. None of us will know how to say "bathroom" in Spanish. The town will look like a running sore and we'll drive another four hours for someplace to stay. Then the car will start hemorrhaging—

Stop, said her friend. It all sounds so enchanting, I have to restrain myself from leaping behind the wheel.

Maybe we should aim for Disneyland instead, said the strange man. More our speed. How about you, Catherine, want to break a bottle of champagne over the fender? Get us off to a proper start?

So she had a name after all. It seemed to shrink her further into manageable dimensions, like knowing the name of the disease you were suffering from. Catherine removed her hand from her cheek and spoke in a small, matter-of-fact voice: No, I can't take any vacation time before June. Besides, I don't like champagne.

Said like a true party-pooper, she thought. Again she felt her own power; at that moment it was dizzying, she had to rein it in. But first she allowed herself one smile at her lover, open and challenging, as if forcing him to acknowledge that power, her smooth hair catching the light, the grace of her moving hands. He smiled back, though he couldn't help looking a little furtive. She felt a touch of scorn for him then.

Of course neither that nor her confidence lasted very long. She and her friend had to leave, and as they stood exchanging good-byes, Catherine bent towards her lover, about to tell him something. That soft, placid face might have its own appeal, she realized, a wistful and sedate beauty. She arrived home depressed, and with hiccups she couldn't get rid of.

The next time she saw her lover she said I hope you weren't too uncomfortable the other day. I guess it was inevitable we'd have to suffer through that scene sometime.

He shrugged. I thought you almost enjoyed it.

Maybe I did, she admitted. I could pretend we'd come there together.

He crossed the room and examined the objects on her dresser. From the way he picked them up and replaced them—pencil, ball of yarn, nail file—she could tell he had no idea what they were, what he was doing. The room was dim and his nakedness looked nearly blue.

Of course she had not acknowledged his real meaning: she enjoyed confronting Catherine, however indirectly. She only wished she were a stage villainess, able to resort to outlandish weapons. Anything, she thought, was easier than putting things into words, asking him to choose between them. So she lay back on the pillows, her silence a demand and a reproach.

Would he speak? The issues between them seemed to have congealed. He sat on the edge of the bed, and, without looking at her, rested one hand on her stomach. She shuddered a little at its careless weight, the ticking of nerves he evoked so easily. It's hard, he began, to get yourself out of certain situations. Even when there are good reasons to.

She stared, but his face was still averted. It was the most general of openings. Who was he talking about? What situation?

You see, Catherine and I—he stammered a bit over the name and her own tongue seemed to go dead in her mouth—it's not that things are always that great for us. Of course you don't know her, but she can be entirely unreasonable. Sometimes she gets into these states . . . temper tantrums, I don't know what else to call them. She'll come after me with both hands. He smiled briefly. I know that's hard to imagine, looking at her.

No, she thought, not really, it made absolute sense, put her picture of Catherine into perspective. All that sullenness catalyzed. Fighting was their metaphor, had been right from the start.

He was waiting for her response; when she made none it seemed to disconcert him. Maybe I'm getting old, he said. I mean, maybe you realize that everything is imperfect, a compromise, and you're willing to settle for less.

She wanted to scream What are you trying to say? but the pressure of his hand kept her silent.

But anybody you've been with that long . . . he was floundering, apologizing for his weakness, begging her to finish things for him.

Had she waited all this time to hear something so commonplace as this? That he found it impossible to leave Catherine? She was answered by the cold judgmental voice she'd stifled for so long, saying What else did you expect? What else did you ever think would happen? She was gripped by such a fury of revulsion, for him, for herself, surely he must feel it through her skin. But his eyes showed only shame and anxiety.

I understand how things have to be, she said, speaking slowly, trying to buy herself time to think. She was afraid that his next words would be We can't keep seeing each other, it's too risky, too sad, too painful. She had avoided words because they cut you loose so easily. One more breath and she'd be entirely adrift. So she said Anyway, I've been thinking of leaving town. As she spoke it became true.

He looked genuinely startled. Why? Where are you going?
Mexico, she couldn't resist saying. No. Actually—and she detailed the standing offer of a friend in California. Come out any
time, there was a spare bedroom, fine weather, a terrace with lemon
trees, an offer she'd never seriously considered until now. She
finished speaking and waited for him to talk her out of it or say he
was coming with her. Of course he wouldn't and she wouldn't beg
him. It occurred to her she had entirely the wrong sort of pride.

What he said was I should know better than to try and change
your mind about anything. You're the strongest woman I know.

Musclebound, she heard herself saying, wondering where her terrible flippancy came from. Musclebound between the ears. She was
thinking, Strong? Would either of them ever see what the other did?

I'll miss you, he said. How easily they seemed to be letting each
other go! Now he embraced her, he was hot and blind, she felt herself pushed to the very edges of the bed. This, their lovemaking, was
something he would never let go or refuse, that was why it was all she
offered to him. His breath rasped across her ear, he was
saying—love—I love you. What was that, she thought, a word,
another word. She tried to maintain her anger, even turn it to contempt, telling herself she had expected some braver decision from
him, some victory of passion over habit. But in the end she whis-
pered back to him, love, yes, she loved him, using the word extravagantly. And maybe this was love and she had gone about it all
wrong.

You're beautiful, she said afterwards. You look like those paint-
ings of Christ after he's been taken down from the cross.

He opened his eyes. You do say the oddest things.

Do I? She tugged at a thick lock of his hair. Let's not make this
the last time.

Oh no. Definitely not the last. When are you going to California?

Not right away. I haven't made any definite plans. She felt light-
headed, echoing with irony. Kits, cats, sacks, wives, how many were
going to St. Ives? The answer, which had always eluded her: One.

This time it was he who began the game. They sat crosslegged on
the mattress, resting their fists on their knees. She seemed to win
without effort, rock to his scissors, paper to his rock, scissors to his

paper, and he exclaimed in mock annoyance. Perhaps she really could read his mind now. Or perhaps, she thought, she was seeing the laws by which those shapes moved. Perhaps they were herself, him, and Catherine, each able to damage the other, each combination causing loss. Though who stood for what? Nothing was ever that precise.

It was raining, of course, when he had to go, a thin black rain in the early winter darkness. She allowed herself to imagine the heat and brilliance of California skies. She allowed herself to imagine some perfect balance of love, some working anatomical model where blood looped smoothly between head and heart.

He was lingering at the door, hesitant, mournful, beautiful as a wound in perfect flesh can be beautiful. Perhaps, in spite of what they'd said, this was indeed their last time. Instead of embracing him she smiled and pressed her open hand against his, palm to palm, paper kissing paper.

Applause, Applause

Poor Bernie, Ted thought, as rain thudded against the car like rotten fruit. Watching it stream and bubble on the windshield he promised himself not to complain about it lest Bernie's feelings be hurt. He was anxious to impress this on his wife. Poor Bernie, he said aloud. Things never work out the way he plans.

His wife nodded. Ted could see from her unsmiling, preoccupied face that it would be difficult to coax her into a conspiracy. In fact, she was probably blaming him for it: his friend, his weekend, therefore, his rain. Look, Ted said. He went to so much trouble setting this up. I'd hate to have him think we weren't enjoying it, whatever happens.

Lee, his wife, turned her chin toward him. He used to call her the Siennese Madonna because of that narrow face, long cheeks and haughty blue eyes. Easy to see her reduced to two-dimensional paint. She had never heard of Sienna. Now she said All right, I won't sulk. But I'll save the vivaciousness till later, OK?

He was a little hurt that she saw no need to be charming for him, but he said nothing. After all, she hadn't complained. He burrowed his hands in his pockets for warmth and looked out the smeared window.

The car was parked in a clearing of pebbled yellow clay. On all sides were dark sopping pine trees, impenetrable, suffocating. It made him a little dizzy to think of how limitless those trees were, how many square miles they covered. The clearing contained two gas pumps and a trading post that sold moccasins, orange pop, and insect repellant. If you turned your back on the building it was easy to believe the world contained only the pines and the implacable rain.

Poor Bernie. He wondered at what point the friends of one's youth acquire epithets. When do we begin to measure their achievements against their ambitions?

Ten years ago he and Bernie Doyle were in college. Ten years ago they sat in bars, Bernie's pipe smoke looped around their heads. Or perhaps on the broken-spined, cat-perfumed sofa that was always reincarnated in their succession of apartments. How they had talked: God, he had never talked that seriously, that openly, to a woman. Perhaps it was something one outgrew. Like the daydreams of the dusky, moody photographs that would appear on one's book jackets. The experimentation with names. Theodore Valentine? T. R. Valentine? T. Robert Valentine? The imaginary interviews. ("Valentine is a disarmingly candid, intensely personal man whose lean, somber features belie his formidable humor. The day I met him he wore an old black turtleneck, Levis and sandals, a singularly unpretentious yet becoming costume . . . ")

Yes, he had admitted all these fantasies to Bernie, and Bernie admitted he shared them. How vulnerable they had been to each other, still were, he supposed. Behind the naive vanities, the daydreams, they had very badly wanted to be writers. Had wanted it without knowing at all what it was they wanted, their fervor making up for their ignorance. His older self was cooler, more noncommittal, for he had learned that to publicize your goals means running the risk of falling short of them.

Ten years of letters, of extravagant alcoholic phone calls. The continual measure they took of each other. Their vanished precocity, reluctantly cast aside at age twenty-five or so. Ten years which established Ted's increasingly self-conscious, increasingly offhand reports of publications, recognitions. Bernie had kept up for a few years, had even talked about getting a book together. After that he responded to Ted's letters with the same grave formula: he wasn't getting a lot done but he hoped to have more time soon. Ted was sure he'd given it up entirely. He knew how easy it was to let your discipline go slack. You had to drive yourself continually, not just to get the work done but to keep faith. Faith that what you were doing was worth the hideous effort you put into it. Easier, much easier, to let it go. The whole process of writing was a road as quirky and blind as the one they had driven this morning to the heart of the Adirondacks, this weekend, and the epithet, Poor Bernie.

Was he himself a success? He wasn't able to say that, not yet at least. Three years ago a national magazine printed a story. The smaller quarterlies published him with some regularity, paid him less frequently. His was one of the names an extremely well-read person might frown at and say Yes, I think I've heard of him. It was like being one of those Presidents no one can ever remember, Polk or Millard Fillmore. Of course you wanted more than that.

But he'd made progress. He hadn't given up. These were the important things. And he dreaded the inevitable discussions with Bernie when their younger incarnations would stand in judgment of them. How could he manage to be both tactful and truthful, feeling as he did that uncomfortable mixture of protectiveness and contempt. Yes, he admitted it, the slightest touch of contempt . . .

Is this them, Lee asked as an orange VW station wagon, its rain-slick paint lurid against the pines, slowed at the clearing. Ted squinted. Maybe . . . The car stopping. Yeah, I think so. The window on the passenger's side was rolled down and a woman's face bobbed and smiled at him. He had an impression of freckles, skin pink as soap. Paula? Ted grinned and pantomimed comprehension.

We're supposed to follow, he told Lee, and eased the car onto the road. Again the dripping trees closed over them. They were climbing now, trailing the VW along a tight spiral. It was impossible to see more than twenty yards ahead. At times they passed mailboxes, or shallow openings in the woods that indicated roads, but for the most part there was only the green-black forest, the thick pudding rain.

Where's that college he teaches at, asked Lee. Ted looked at her and tried to unravel the history of her thoughts for the last silent half-hour. She still wore her languid, neutral expression. The Madonna attends a required meeting of the Ladies' Auxiliary.

Sixty miles away. No, farther. Eighty. It was another thing he wondered about, Bernie's precarious instructor job. Four sections of composition. Abortion, Pro and Con. My First Date. Topic sentences. Footnotes.

And he married one of his students?

Ted nodded. It was hard for him to imagine Bernie as a figure of authority or some little girl regarding him with the reverence and hysteria of student crushes. But it had happened.

Lee pointed. The VW's bumper was winking at them and Ted slowed, ready to turn. Now it was scarcely a road they followed but a dirt lane. Milder, deciduous trees interlaced above them and screened the rain somewhat. They rocked along the muddy ruts for half a mile.

Then the sudden end of the lane, the cabin of dark brown shingles with Bernie already waving from the porch. Ted was out of the car almost before it had stopped, was shaking Bernie's hand and saying something like Son of a gun, and grinning. Bernie said Valentine, you lout, and reached up to pound him on the back.

The women drifted after them. Hey Paula, come shake hands with Ted. And this is Lee. Bernie, Paula. Ted found himself appraising Lee as she climbed the steps, took satisfaction in her length of leg, her severely beautiful face now softened with a smile. The four of them stood nodding at each other for a moment. Like two sets of dolls built to different scale, Ted thought, the Doyles so small, he and Lee an angular six inches taller. Furious exercise had kept Ted in shape, and he knew the faint line of sunburn under his eyes was becoming. He realized he was standing at attention, and cursed his vanity.

Bernie looked more than ever like a Swiss toymaker as imagined by Walt Disney. Small bones and white supple hands. His gray eyes unfocused behind rimless glasses. The ever-present pipe which, when inserted, drew his whole face into a preoccupied, constipated look. He had grown a dark manicured beard.

And Paula? He knew her to be at least twenty-four, but she could have passed for sweet eighteen. Snub little nose. Smiling mouth like the squiggle painted on a china doll. Green eyes in that pink transparent skin. Yes, she would be something to take notice of in a stuffy classroom.

Even as he absorbed and ordered his impressions the group broke, Bernie pushing the front door open, Paula talking about food. He followed Bernie into a paneled room and the damp, bone-deep cold that would accompany the whole weekend first seized him. He heard Lee's lightly inflected voice keeping her promise: What a lovely fireplace. We can tell ghost stories around it.

You bet, said Bernie, and squatted before it, poking the grate. There's even dry wood on the porch.

Looking at him, Ted experienced the uneasy process of having to square his observations with his memories. As if this was not really Bernie until he conformed with Ted's image of him. How long had it been, three years? He began to be more sure of himself as he noted familiar mannerisms surfacing. Bernie's solemnity; he discussed firewood in the same tone another man might use for religion. The deftness of his hands wielding the fireplace tools. Ted imagined him shaping chunks of pine into cuckoo clocks, bears, and monkeys . . .

Now stop that, he warned himself. It was a writer's curse, this verbal embroidery. Never seeing anything as it was, always analyzing and reformulating it. Maybe the entire habit of observation, the thing he trained himself in, was just a nervous tic, a compulsion. He shook his head and joined Lee in her exploration of the cabin.

The main room was high-ceilinged, dark. In hot weather he imagined its shadows would bless the skin, but now the bare floors made his feet ache with cold. There were two bedrooms, one on each side of the main room. The furniture was a mixture of wicker and raw wood. In the rear were a trim new kitchen and bathroom. They stepped out the back door and Ted whistled.

Even in the rain the blue-gray bowl of the lake freshened his eyes. Its irregular shoreline formed bays, coves, little tongues of land, all furred with silent pine. He could not see the opposite shore. There was an island just where he might have wished for one, a mound of brush and rock. The air smelled clean and thin.

Lee spoke to Bernie, who had joined them. It's incredible. Just too lovely.

Bernie grinned, as if the lake were a treat he had prepared especially for them. And Ted felt all his discomfort drop away as he saw his friend's happiness, his desire to make them happy. God bless

Bernie; he'd forget all this gloomy nonsense about artistic accomplishment. Are there many cabins up here, he asked.

Quite a few. But the lake is so big and the trees so thick we have a lot of privacy. He pointed with his pipe. There's the boathouse. And dock. No beach I'm afraid, it's all mud.

They stood in the shelter of the porch, rain hanging like lace from the gutters. Then Lee said Too cold out here for me, and they all went inside.

Paula was rummaging through groceries in the kitchen. Here, said Lee. Let me do something useful. A little cluster of polite words filled the air, Paula demurring, Lee insisting. Ted hoped that for once Lee would be graceful about helping in the kitchen, leave him and Bernie alone without getting sarcastic later about Man-Talk and Woman's Work. He tried to catch her eye but she was pulling her blonde hair into a knot and asking Paula about the mayonnaise.

Bernie offered him a beer and they drifted to the living room. Sitting down Ted had a moment of apprehension, like the beginning of a job interview. Bernie frowned and coaxed his pipe into life. How often had he used it as a prop; Ted knew his shyness. At last the bowl reddened. So tell me, Bernie said. How goes it with you?

Ted realized how much he'd rehearsed his answer: Not too bad. But I'll never be rich.

Bernie chuckled. Poor but honest.

Poor but poor. With Lee's job we get by. And I do some free-lancing, write ad copy for a car dealer, that sort of thing. He shrugged. And how about you?

Ted was aware he had shifted too quickly, had seemed to brush off Bernie's question in an attempt to be polite, reciprocal. Damn. He'd have to watch that.

Ah, Bernie said. The pastoral life of a college instructor. It's like being a country priest, really, with your life revolving around the feast days. Registration. Final exams. Department meetings on First Fridays.

You're getting tired of it?

It's a job, Ted. Like anything else it has its ups and downs. Actually I'm glad it's not excessively glamorous. This way I don't feel tied to it, committed. I can stay fluid, you know?

What would you do instead?

Sell hardware. Open a museum. I don't know. Paula wants to work as a photographer. She's pretty good. And I wouldn't mind getting back to the writing. It's been simmering in me for a long time.

That hint of justification. Ted felt the same prepared quality in Bernie's answer as in his own. He risked his question: Have you been able to get anything done?

Any writing, you mean? Dribs and drabs. I decided what I needed was to remove myself from pressure, you know? Work at my own pace without worrying about marketing a finished product. Of course I know that's not the way you go about it.

Yeah. It's out of the typewriter and into the mails.

You still work on a schedule?

Absolutely. Seems to be the only way I get anything done. Lee covers for me. I have tantrums if the phone rings.

You must really throw yourself into the thing.

The implied sympathy, the chance to speak of his frustrations with someone who would understand them, was a luxury. Jesus, he said. You spend hours wrestling with yourself, trying to keep your vision intact, your intensity undiminished. Sometimes I have to stick my head under the tap to get my wits back. And for what? You know what publishing is like these days. Paper costs going up all the time. Nothing gets printed unless it can be made into a movie. Everything is media. Crooked politicians sell their unwritten memoirs for thousands. I've got a great idea for a novel. It's about a giant shark who's possessed by a demon while swimming in the Bermuda Triangle. And the demon talks in CB lingo, see? There'll be recipes in the back.

Bernie laughed and Ted continued. Then the quarterlies, the places you expect to publish serious writing. They're falling all over themselves trying to be trendy, avant-garde. If you write in sentence fragments and leave plenty of blank space on the page, you're in. Pretentiousness disguised as trail-blazing. All the editors want to set themselves up as interpreters of a new movement. I hope they choke on their own jargon. Anti-meta-post-contemporary-surfictional literature. Balls.

He stopped for breath. I'm sorry, he said. Didn't mean to get carried away.

Not at all. It does me good to hear a tirade now and then. Reminds me of college, makes me feel ten years younger.

Still. He should not have spoken with such bitterness. It sounded like he was making excuses. Ted smiled, lightening his tone. The artist takes his lonely stand against the world.

As well he ought to. But really, Valentine, don't you get tired of beating your head against all that commercialism? Trying to compete with it? I mean, of course you do, but do you think it affects what you write?

Was it Bernie's solemnity that always made his questions sound so judgmental? Ted knew it was more than an issue of mannerisms. Bernie pondered things, thought them through; you respected his sincerity. Ted gave the only answer pride allowed: No, because the work can't exist in a vacuum. It has to get out there in the world, and reach people. Ted drained his beer and ventured to define the issue between them. You're saying it's better to be an Emily Dickinson, a violet by a mossy stone half-hidden to the eye, that sort of thing. Keep it in shoeboxes in the closet so you can remain uncorrupted.

Bernie turned his hands palms upward and managed to express dissent by spreading his white fingers. Just that it's possible to lose sight of what you set out to do. Even get too discouraged.

How quickly we've moved into position, Ted thought. Each of us defending our lives. He remembered his earlier resolution to speak tactfully, cushion any comparison between their accomplishments. And here was Bernie seeming to demand such comparison. How easy it would be to make some mention of his publications, play up some of the things he'd muted in his letters, insist on Bernie's paying tribute to them. He even admitted to himself that beneath everything he'd wanted his success acknowledged. Like the high school loser who dreams of driving to the class reunion in a custom-made sports car. As if only those who knew your earlier weakness could verify your success.

But he would not indulge himself. Partly because, like his earlier outburst, it would threaten to say too much, and partly because he wanted this meeting to be without friction. Couldn't they rediscover their younger, untried selves? It was a kind of nostalgia. So he said I don't know, Bernie. You may be right. But the only way for me to accomplish anything is by competing with the market.

Bernie considered this, seemed to accept it as a final statement. He dumped his pipe into the fireplace. Ted noticed the beginning of a tonsure, a doorknob-sized patch of naked scalp. The sight enabled him to recapture all his tenderness. Shall we join the ladies, Bernie asked, rising.

They were sitting at the kitchen table with mugs of coffee. Well, Ted said, resting a hand on Lee's shoulder. I hope you haven't been bored. He meant it half as apology, half as warning: you'd better not be.

Au contraire, Lee answered. We've been trying to reconcile post-Hegelian dogma with Jamesian pragmatism. But she grinned.

And Paula said Actually, we were telling raunchy jokes. Give us ten more minutes.

He liked her. Her pinkness, plumpness. Like a neat little bird, all smooth lines and down. Her round good-humored chin. And Lee seemed to be doing all right with her.

I think it's quit raining, said Bernie. If you've got sturdy enough shoes we could take a hike.

It was still very wet under the trees. A careless tug at a branch might flip cold rainbow-edged drops down your back. And the sky was gray as concrete. But they enjoyed the silence, the soft sucking ground matted with last year's needles. They perched on a fallen tree at the lake's edge and chunked stones into the crisp water. Bernie explained it was too early, too cool for the black flies whose bites made bloody circles just beneath the skin.

How often do you get up here, Ted asked. Bernie told him about every other weekend when the weather was right. Ted launched into abundant, envious speech: They were lucky sons-of-bitches, did they know that back in Illinois there were only tame little man-made lakes, tidy parks, lines of Winnebagoes like an elephant graveyard, right Lee? As if complimenting this part of Bernie's life might restore some balance between them.

They walked back single file along the sunken trail. Ted was at the rear. Lee's blondeness looked whiter, milkier out here. Perhaps it was the heaviness of the dark green air, like the light just before a thunderstorm which plays up contrasts. Bernie and Paula's heads were the same shade of sleek brown, slipping in and out of his vision. It struck him that once again he was observing and being consious of himself as an observer. It was a habit he'd fallen into, not necessarily a bad one. But he'd been working very hard at the writing lately (Lee had insisted on this vacation; he rather begrudged the time spent away from his desk) and this heightened self-awareness was a sign of strain. As if he couldn't really escape his work or the persona that went with it.

The Artist's impressions of a walk in the woods. The Artist's view on viewing. The Artist on Art. How do you get your ideas for stories, Mr. Valentine? Well, I simply exploit everything I come into contact with. One ended, of course, by losing all spontaneity. You saw people as characters, sunsets as an excuse for similes—

Bernie called a warning over his shoulder just as Ted felt a drop of rain slide down his nose. They quickened their pace to a trot as the rain fell, first in fat splatters that landed as heavily as frogs, then finer, harder. By the time they reached the porch their clothes were dark and dripping.

Fire, said Bernie. Coffee and hot baths, said Paula. The movement, the busyness, cheered them as much as the dry clothes. When at last they sat on each side of the stone fireplace, the odor of smoke working into their skins and hair, they all felt the same sense of shelter.

Damn, said Bernie. I wanted to take you fishing. But he looked comfortable, his pipe bobbing in his mouth.

Maybe tomorrow, said Paula. The rain had polished her skin, now the fire was warming it, bringing out different tints: apricot, cameo. She and Bernie made a peaceful, domestic couple. He could imagine them sitting like this, on either side of the fire, for the next thirty years. The retired Swiss toymaker and his wife.

But was Bernie happy? Did he feel, as Ted would have in his

place, a sense of failure, of goals having shrunk. You never knew. Or, this visit would probably not allow him to learn. The time was too short to break down much of the politeness that passed between them as guest and host. Recapturing their former intimacy, that intensity, seemed as difficult as remembering what virginity had felt like. They should have left the wives behind, just come up here for a messy bachelor weekend of drinking and cards. This impulse moved him to ask if anyone wanted a whiskey.

They did. He passed glasses, leaned back into his chair. Well, said Lee. It's too early to tell ghost stories.

Ted and I could talk about our misspent youth.

She wants something ghostly, Doyle, not ghastly.

Oh go ahead, Lee urged Bernie. Tell me something that can be used against him. She was at her most animated, perhaps from the first bite of the liquor. The Madonna is photographed for a Seagram's commercial. Go ahead, she repeated.

Tell her I was a football hero.

If you won't tell Paula about that indecent exposure thing.

Agreed. Ted gulped at his drink to induce the mood of nostalgia. One thing I'll always remember. You and me taking a bottle of strawberry wine up on the roof of the humanities building.

Did you really, said Paula.

We thought we were Bohemians, Bernie explained. Artistic, not ethnic.

We pretended it was absinthe.

A rooftop in Paris at the turn of the century.

I was James Joyce.

I was Oscar Wilde.

We were going to be paperback sensations.

We were full of shit.

I don't know, Ted objected. I mean, certainly we were naive. Who isn't at twenty? But you have to begin with wild idealism, dreams of glory. It's the raw fuel that gets you through the disappointments.

You mean the brute facts of editors, publishing.

Ted nodded. The manuscripts that come back stained with spaghetti sauce. The places that misspell your name. All the ambiguities of success. If we'd known what was actually involved in writing, we probably never would have attempted it.

When we leave here, Lee put in, we have to go to New York and talk with Ted's agent. You wouldn't believe the nastiness and wheeler-dealer stuff that goes on in that New York scene. It's like a court in Renaissance Italy. Intrigues within intrigues.

Bernie raised his eyebrows above the rims of his glasses. You have an agent now?

Yes. Since last November. He's trying to place the novel for me.

And you've finished the novel? Paula, do we have champagne? I've been hearing about this book for years.

Well, I've finished the draft. If it's accepted I'll no doubt have to do rewrites. Damn Lee for bringing up the agent; it would only make Bernie more aware of the gap between their achievements. He searched for some way to de-escalate things. You should be glad you've escaped all this messiness so far. Retained your youthful innocence.

The bottom log of the fire, which had been threatening to burn through, now collapsed. Red winking sparks flew up the black column of the chimney as the fire assumed a new pattern. Bernie squatted in front of it raking the embers into place. He spoke without turning around.

You know, I read that piece you had in—what was it—the one about the schizophrenic?

"The Lunatic." He sat up a little straighter in his chair, adopted the carefully pleasant expression with which he received criticism.

Ted was very happy with that piece, Lee informed everyone. And the magazine did a good production job. She beamed at him, sweetly proud of making a contribution to the discussion. He wished she hadn't spoken, had left him free to frame his reply after listening to Bernie. But she was only repeating what she'd heard him say.

That's it, "The Lunatic." I admire the language use, the control in the thing. The way you managed to milk images. But—

that terrible pause—

I felt there was a kind of slickness in the thing, almost glibness. I mean, you're talking about a man who's having a mental breakdown. And you treat that rather flippantly. Perhaps you intended it, but I wondered why.

There were a number of replies he could make. He settled for the most general: The story is something of a satire, Bernie. Think of all the literature that's dealt with madness. It's an extremely well-trodden path. You simply can't write about the subject straightforwardly anymore. People expect something new.

Bernie frowned and rubbed his jaw under the dense beard. Ted knew, watching him, that Bernie had thought his argument through. Had prepared it carefully, step by step, like he did everything.

I thought, Bernie continued, that your complaint against avant-garde fiction was its emphasis on form over content. Blank space on the page, tortured syntax, that sort of thing. The writing screaming for attention. Aren't you agreeing with them now? Saying, in effect, rather than exploring the individuality of this character or situation, I'll dress it up in a different package. Pretend not to take it seriously.

Both women were watching rather helplessly, as if they realized their little store of soothing words and social graces would be of no use. And the defense that came to Ted's mind (Nobody writes like Henry James anymore. Or, more crudely, Your aesthetic is outdated) sounded like a small boy's taunts. So he said I do take the character and situation seriously. That doesn't mean one can't experiment with form, depart from rigid storytelling conventions. Otherwise you wind up repeating what's already been done. Repeating yourself too.

Bernie shook his head. Again that gesture of judgment. I'm sorry, but I see it as a response to the market. The thing I was talking about earlier. You tailor the writing to what the editors are buying. Maybe unconsciously. You're certainly not writing about the giant sharks. But it's still a form of corruption.

And what, in particular, is being corrupted?

I hope I can put this right. It's like, that increased self-consciousness, that authorial presence that's always thrusting itself between the reader and the page—see, I'm telling this story, you're reading it, I'll try to amuse you, watch this—is rather paralyzing. What you're doing, a general you (a parenthetical smile), is making disclaimers for the piece, covering your tracks. I'll play this a little tongue-in-cheek so I won't be called to account for it.

You might as well dispute abstraction in painting, Bernie. Form can't be entirely neglected in favor of content. Otherwise we might still be seeing those Victorian pictures of blind children and noble hounds.

It runs the danger of shallowness, Ted.

Well, I suppose the only way to avoid the dangers is not to write anything at all.

He hadn't realized how angry he was until he heard himself speak. Damn the whiskey, damn his own thin-skinned hatred of criticism. He was too quick to take things as insults. Now, having said the one unforgivable thing, there was no retreat. The four of them sat without looking at each other. Bernie plunged into a fury of pipe-cleaning, tamping, lighting, as another man might have cracked his knuckles. The rain filled the silence, gusting against the windows and shrinking the warmth of the fire.

Finally Paula said I'm going to see what there is for dinner. Ted stood up as soon as she did, muttering about another drink. He paused in the kitchen only long enough to slosh the liquor in his glass. Paula opened the refrigerator and said Hm, fried chicken maybe? He said Fine and walked out the back door.

The rain had brought an early blue darkness. He could still make out the shoreline, the agitation of the lake as the rain pocked its surface. Far away on his left shone one point of light, a white feeble thing that he could not imagine indicated human companionship, laughter, warmth. Even though he stood under the ledge, moisture beaded his clothes like dew. He gave himself over completely to the melancholy of it all. The only consolation he could find was the thought that argument was a form of intimacy.

When he came back inside both women were busy in the kitchen. Can I peel potatoes or something, he asked. They sat him at the kitchen table with a bowl of strawberries to hull. A little boy hiding behind women. He didn't want to go back to the living room where he knew Bernie would be sitting. Lee and Paula seemed determined to speak of nothing more serious than gravy making. He watched Lee as she moved between stove and sink, a little surprised at her vivacity. As if she had formed some alliance without his being aware of it. Her hair had dried in soft waves with a hint of fuzziness; a looser style than she usually wore. Although she spoke to him occasionally, she did not meet his eye. It didn't seem that she was avoiding him; rather, she was busy, he was extraneous, incidental . . .

But he was projecting his injured feeling onto her, his gloom and self-pity. Snap out of it, he told himself. You're going to be here another thirty-six hours.

That realization must have been shared, must have been what got them through the evening. The act of sitting down to food together restored some tenuous rhythm. Afterward Paula suggested Monopoly. They let the bright cardboard, the little mock triumphs and defeats, absorb them. Ted thought how harmless all greed and competition were when reduced to this scale, then he berated himself for facile irony.

At midnight Bernie yawned and said I'm down to thirty dollars and Marvin Gardens. Somebody buy me out.

Who's ahead? Add it up, Paula suggested.

It turned out to be Ted, who felt hulking and foolish raking in his pile of paper money. Flimsy pastel trophies. He was duly congratulated. He did a parody of the young Lindbergh acknowledging cheers. Modestly tugging his forelock. The tycoon needs some rest, he said, and they all agreed.

Goodnight. Goodnight, and if you need extra blankets they're at the top of the closet. I'm sure we'll be fine. Bernie latched the door and said Maybe it'll clear up tomorrow.

It took Ted a moment to realize he was speaking of the rain.

He waited until everyone was settled before he used the bathroom. No use risking more sprightly greetings. When he got back Lee was in bed, her fair hair spilling from the rolled sheets like corn silk.

He wanted her to start talking first, but her eyes were squeezed shut against the bed-side lamp. Well, he said. Too neutral, inadequate.

Would you turn that light off?

He reached, produced darkness. She sighed and said Much better. He lay for a moment accustoming himself to the black stillness, the smell of the rough pine boards. The mattress was sparse, lopsided. It seemed to have absorbed the dank cold of the cabin. He burrowed into its thin center. Then the even sound of Lee's breathing told him she was falling asleep. Almost angry, he shook her shoulder.

What? She was more irritated than sleepy.

Don't fall asleep. I wanted to talk to you.

Go ahead.

He waited a moment to control himself. You're not making it very easy.

She twisted inside the sheets until she rested on one elbow, facing him. All right, I'll make it easy. What the hell were you arguing about? I hate it when you start talking like that. All that rhetoric. You take it so seriously. Was any of it worth snapping at him like that?

Of course I take it seriously. He was accusing me of shallowness. Corruption.

Oh boy. Lee drawled her sarcasm. And you couldn't forget your literary reflexes for one minute.

No. I guess I couldn't.

Her hand emerged from the darkness and gave his shoulder a series of small tentative pats. Poor Ted. Her voice was kinder. The pats continued, light but persistent, as if a moth were battering itself against him. He supressed the impulse to brush it away.

Why poor Ted?

Because sometimes I think you don't enjoy what you're doing at all. The writing I mean. You get so upset.

Don't be silly.

I know. The Agony and the Ecstasy. She yawned. Well I hope you two make up. They're nice folks.

Her lips, seeming disembodied in the blind darkness, found his chin, his mouth. Good night.

Good night.

He waited until she was asleep or pretending to be asleep. He got up, put on his pants and sweater, and padded into the kitchen. Turned on the fluorescent light over the sink.

Her cruelest words spoken in her softest voice. Her revenge, thinking or unthinking, for all the times he'd shut himself away from her. He'd had his work to do. His sulks and tantrums. His insistence on the loftiness of his purpose, the promise of his future. His monstrous self-importance. The whole edifice threatened.

He didn't enjoy it.

Of course you were gratified at the high points. The little recognitions and deference. Of course you made a point of bemoaning the labor involved. Saying it drove you mad with frustration. That was expected. But enjoyment? Where was the enjoyment?

The pines still rattled in the wind. The rain was a dim silver fabric without seam or edge, unrolling from the sky. He thought of walking into it, losing himself in all that fragrant blackness, in the thick gunmetal lake. Oh he was tired of his cleverness, his swollen sensitivity. Better to crouch under a rock in the rain and reduce yourself to nerve, skin, and muscle. But his self-consciousness would not allow this either. It told him it would be melodramatic, a petulant gesture. Bad form.

Something, some weight, passed over the floorboards behind him and he turned, his nostrils cocked. It was the ticklish perfume of pipe smoke that reached him first.

H'lo, he said, and Bernie's mouth curved around the polished wooden stem of his pipe. He managed to walk to where Ted was standing by the back door without seeming to advance in a straight line.

Foul weather, he said nodding. He too had resumed his clothes.

I'll say. They watched the faint movement of water on water. Then Bernie said Drink?

Sure.

While there was still tension perceptible in their cautious responses, in Bernie's stiff-wristed pouring of drinks, it seemed a formality. The simple fact of coming together like this was a promise of reconciliation. When Bernie was seated across from him, Ted began with the obvious. I'm sorry about tonight. I was way out of line.

I guess I provoked you, Ted. I'm jealous. I admit it.

And I am insecure and narcissistic.

Would it be too maudlin to wish we were kids again?

Ted shook his head. In some ways I think I'm still twenty. The prize student who's always fawning for approval, pats on the head.

You're too hard on yourself.

Yes. I am. He blinked at the checked tablecloth, trying to get his eyes to focus on its pattern.

And I'm not hard enough. Bernie smiled. Such confessions.

They're necessary. Who else can absolve us of our sordid pasts?

Now the room has the contours and atmosphere of all rooms in which people stay awake talking. The fluorescent light is grainy, staring. The clutter on the kitchen table—ketchup bottle, sagging butter dish, tin of Nestle's Quik, the rowdy crudded ashtray—the world is narrowed into these, a little universe that the eyes return to again and again. Now it begins, the sorting and testing of words. Remember that words are not symbols of other words. There are words which, when tinkered with, become honest representatives of the cresting blood, the fine living net of nerves. Define rain. Or even joy. It can be done.

Driving to Oregon

Friends sent them one of those postcards produced by the same technicians who can make a Kansas Holiday Inn suggest a palmy oasis. This time the process had resulted in overkill. Inflamed, tomato-colored wildflowers were grafted to a background of turquoise lake and emerald pines. One white, cone-shaped mountain rose in a sky so densely blue it resembled the paste-waxed fender of a new car. Bert and Mary Ann Lilly taped the card to the refrigerator. When their friends came back they said:

Pretty? That's not the word. Beautiful. Gorgeous. Better than that. Up in the mountains it's cool even in summer, with all that pine smell. Deer, oh yeah, we saw plenty deer. Down in the valleys are orchards. Apricot, cherry, pear. You can pick wild blackberries. And the rivers. What was that big slow one, the color of a green apple? The Umpqua. The Alsea. Waterfalls. People graze horses along the banks. And we haven't even begun to tell you about the coast.

Bert and Mary Ann smiled at each other with one corner of their mouths sucked in, meaning, Some people have all the luck. Man, said Bert, why wasn't I born there? The only deer I ever seen is Bambi.

Waterfalls, huh? said Mary Ann, and chewed for a moment on one of her lank, light-brown pigtails. I've never even been out of crummy old Illi-*noy*. Except for Indiana.

You been to St. Louis, Bert reminded her.

Oh, excuse me, St. Louis. Yeah I guess I have been around.

Everyone laughed and Bert shook the plastic bag of marijuana, pinched off enough to fill the pipe bowl.

That's another thing, the friends said. In Oregon you get busted with under an ounce, it's like a parking ticket. No shit.

You guys tryin to make it hard on me? asked Bert. Like you got to keep reminding me what's out there? He flung his hand toward the window and it tangled in the curtains.

Out there beyond the aluminum-sided bungalow with its frill of dusty grass: Decatur, Illinois.

> Beans. Soybeans.
> You get em from the Staley Plant.

Beantown. Staley Soybean, right squat in the middle of the city. The highway arches over it. A panorama of webbed pipes, giant tanks, chimneys throwing dirty blond smoke into the air. Like driving into a huge stinking motor. Now, at harvest time, trucks rock through the streets, spilling hard wrinkled little beans into the gutters. What do they make out of them, shoe polish? Bug killer? Jesus, how can anything that's supposed to be food smell so bad?

Always plenty of cooking oil in the stores.

Now, in August, the big shallow man-made lake is drying up, showing its bottom of yellow mud. The sky is hazy windless blue. A wooly heat clogs the skin.

At night the sidewalks are still hot enough to sting your feet. Downtown, above the squirming pink neon of taverns, rows of black windows. Broken, barred, shuttered, burnt, and empty. Ulcers in the brick.

Honest blight at least makes no pretenses. But farther from the city center, where the town begins to unravel on the prairie, are blocks and blocks of new graceless enterprise. The used car burgers handy pantry discount king liquors. The formica slabs, plate glass and cellophane.

You know what I saw here once, said Mary Ann. A squirrel trying to drag a package of Kraft American Cheese Slices up a tree.

No worse, maybe, than any other small American city. And surely there are blue spring days, shade trees, first snowfalls.

Surely there is some reason we live here. We were born here. We are comfortable with its bland Midwestern sky. Its ugliness has accumulated like rust, stiffening our eyes and hearts. This place

Where Bert drives an hour to run a machine that bags fertilizer, coming home with bitter white dust worked into his dark skin. Fertilizer to grow more of those damn beans.

Where the land is so flat you could see the curve of the earth, if there were anywhere high enough to view it from.

Where the sight of big black Bert and his skinny white wife often stops traffic. Whose Caucasian citizens, noting Mary Ann's pregnancy, are moved to sociologic commentary: A yellow baby with frizzy red hair, that's what she's got in there. Twice as ugly as a plain old nigger. Can you imagine the two of them—makes your skin crawl, don't it.

Not to mention, just yet, what Mary Ann's family said.

Why can't we, asked Mary Ann that night when they were in bed.

Em-oh-en-ee-wy, said Bert. What's got into you? Why all of a sudden we got to move?

For the baby. Her answer so prompt and positive in the dark room. I hated growing up here, you know I did.

She was silent, biting her lips at old grievances. Bert reached out and let her long hair sift through his fingers. You think it makes a difference, being in one place or another? You think it would have made you happier?

Yes.

Well, said Bert, you know we can't afford it now. He kissed her and rolled over into sleep, glad there was something easy and practical to set against her vehemence. But the third time somebody at work rammed his car, they began to talk seriously about it.

After all, it's a free country. Why can't we? Didn't we find each other? Just think of that. Out of this whole world we found each other. I chose you and you me. If we did that we can do anything.

Bert was the oldest of seven children. He watched his brothers and sisters marry, he stood up at their weddings and baby-sat for their kids. Getting fat and going bald early. Good old Uncle Bert. He could see himself in twenty years, grinning over his chins at their grandchildren. Letting them play pat-a-cake on his bare scalp. It wasn't that he had trouble meeting girls, just that none of them stuck. Then at a concert he met Mary Ann. She came home with him that night and never left.

The next morning he drove her to breakfast. I got something to tell you, he said.

She was bent over her pocketbook, looking for a match. Mm? she said.

Her hair was pulled back in a long smooth tail and her skin was pink from the cold morning. How pretty she looked, this moment before he would lose her. I'm twenty-nine years old, he said.

Here's one, she said. Nope. Empty.

Did you hear me? Bert demanded.

Uh huh. I'm nineteen.

I know that. Don't it worry you? I mean, on top of bein black and practically bald—

Oh hush, said Mary Ann. If it'll make you feel better, I got a glass eye. The right one.

Not the first time he'd crossed, been with a white girl. Not the first time for her either. How come you don't wear platform shoes and crazy hats and lavender britches, she asked him when she'd known him for two days. You are the dowdiest black dude I ever saw.

He told her Us fat guys look like walking potatoes in clothes like that. Lavender britches, good Lord, girl.

I don't like those superpimp clothes anyway, she said. But you ain't fat, really.

Or, meeting his family: Gee, they're pretty nice about you bringing home white tail, aren't they?

They traded the car for a pickup with four-wheel drive. You needed something to get around in those mountains, they decided. Bert worked as much overtime as he could that winter. The wind blew stinging dirt across the flatness. Then chunks of filthy ice formed in the gutters, stayed there for weeks. Skin took on the stale, chafed texture of a root left too long in the ground. This is our last winter here, said Bert and Mary Ann. The mercury huddled at the base of the thermometer like frozen blood and they looked at maps and tourist brochures.

From the colorful past to the bustling present, the saga of Oregon is marked by immense natural wealth and beauty. Mighty volcanic peaks overlook the lush coastal plain. A temperate climate makes year-round vacationing popular. See miles of rugged coastline, well-supplied with recreational facilities. Unique opportunities for the sportsman exist, from salmon fishing in crystal streams to stalking antelope in the vast grasslands. Follow the historic Oregon Trail. Magnificent timberland, jewel-like lakes, winding rivers—and more!

I bet folks out west are a lot less prejudiced to blacks, Bert told a friend at work. You know, it being sort of the frontier. Less set in their ways.

Probably, said his friend. They've always got the Indians.

Bert asked him what he meant but his friend said nothing, nothing.

In March the baby was born. They named her Dawn. Lookit that complexion, said Mary Ann. Looks like you didn't have nothing to do with her.

Aw she'll get darker. And she's got a little Afro nose. Hey little girl, pretty girl, don't burp at your daddy.

You're gonna have a pony, Mary Ann told her. Just as soon as those fat little legs are long enough. For they had decided they would live in the country and raise horses.

In June they sold everything but the stereo and a box of kitchen things. How easy it was to strip things away. To discover that once you took the pictures curtains rugs and flowerpots, you were still there. None of it bound you. Leave it behind along with the families, the friends, the lifetime of habit. You were as free and light as the dust balls rolling from one empty room to the next. Dizzy with your own recklessness. You pulled yourself loose and could as easily set down again. Nothing out there you couldn't outwork, outwit, outmaneuver, outlast.

Why can't a little caramel-colored girl-child grow up with a pony in Oregon?

Mary Ann raked through closets, sending tangled coat hangers rattling to the floor. She bruised her knees on suitcases, plunged her uncertain hands into heaps of clothes which she folded and refolded, sorted and resorted. What is the matter with you, Bert demanded after she upset the stack of towels again.

She sat down on the floor, right where she'd been standing. I got to see my folks before we go, she said flatly. Bert started to say something. She held up her hand. I know, I know. But I got to. No I won't take Dawn. You ought to know better than to ask.

He waited for her, crooning to the baby as the summer evening poured through the windows. Blue darkness blurred the corners of the room. In them he saw the vague shapes of his dread.

Evil, blind as a root probing rock, always squirming to reach them.

Something would happen. Even now they would find a way to coax, threaten, or force her.

Evil. You raised your hand to ward it off, but the hand fell away, frail as paper burned to ash. A legacy of malice focused on you. Whispers and warnings. Then the snapping of bone, the wet thick tearing of flesh as the darkie nigger coon got it, got it good.

She would not return. He would stand here all night and the darkness would muffle him, drive him mad. Still he fought with his fear and did not turn on a lamp.

When there was one shining rim of sky left in the west, he heard the truck. It choked and dieseled in the driveway. There was just enough light for him to see her small pale face crossing the room toward him. She pressed against him, hard, and only then began crying. Furious deep tears. The baby, out of fright or hunger, joined in. He held them both, sweet weight, heavy comfort.

Petroleum stink. The flat sun fastened to the hood like an ornament. Concrete, did you ever think there was so much of it? Stale, uniform, wearying: I will multiply thy seeds as the stars of the heaven, and as the concrete which is upon the Interstate.

No matter. It could be ignored, like Iowa, endured, like Nebraska. The tires drummed smoothly, the miles accumulated, tangible, finite. In the back of the pickup their belongings were roped together under taut waterproof canvas, checked at every stop. New maps and new eight-track stereo cartridge tapes that they had not yet grown tired of. A pound of reefer hidden under the seat.

Hey, said Mary Ann. I got an idea. We can get off the Interstate in Wyoming—skewering the map with a fingernail—and go up to Grand Teton or Yellowstone. See?

Bert squinted at the pink and green rectangle that was Wyoming. Aw, that's miles and miles out of our way.

No it ain't. Well maybe a little. But if we stay on 80 we have to go south out of our way. Besides, everything looks the same from the Interstate. I want to see mountains so bad.

It was true. The land had become more open, rolling, as they approached Wyoming. Bleached earth covered with scrub. But the prim green signs equalized everything, made it hard to believe they'd driven a thousand miles. So on their third day from home they turned north, drawn by the names on the map: Green Mountains. Antelope Hills. Sweetwater. Owl Creek.

Bert thought, as the land began to climb, We're doing it. Really doing it. Look, he said, pointing to a sign. Open grazing. Damn, they got cattle traipsing all over the road. He was delighted. I could almost enjoy this, huh?

Uh huh, said Mary Ann, shielding the baby's face from the sun. She could almost enjoy it. Except for something that happened the summer after high school graduation. When a fast-moving full-sized Oldsmobile appeared in the path of her girlfriend's MGB in which she was the third passenger, draped over the gear shift.

Not that she remembered much. Sometimes she tried to recall the exploding glass, the somersault they said she made onto the slick black roof of the Olds. Since she could not remember it she could not forget it, and imagined it in a number of different versions.

Seven weeks she was in a coma. When they were fairly certain she would live, they began to rebuild her face. Wired her mouth shut so the synthetic jawbone and porcelain teeth could get to know each other undisturbed. Inserted a precision-made blue eye into her blind socket. Drew the skin of her neck and scalp forward and sanded it down. Replaced the bony structure of her nose with silicone. Even

took out the bump I used to have, says Mary Ann. Stitched in eyebrows with black surgical thread and planted them with hair.

Mary Ann's mother: Who paid to have you put back together
when you were in twenty-seven pieces? We did, we never gave it a
second thought, we did it because you were our little girl. We did
that for you, doesn't that count for anything?

On her last check-up, two years after the accident, the doctor
agreed to show her photographs that had been taken during the last
phases of surgery. In them you could see the welts, new scar tissue,
but that wasn't so bad.

There were other photographs he refused to show her.

The sound of squealing brakes no longer frightened her. And little
by little she accustomed herself to the feel of a steering wheel sliding
back and forth in her hands.

They had, after all, done an excellent job with the plastic surgery.

Dawn had fallen asleep while nursing. Her small greedy mouth
formed bubbles of milk as she breathed and her face was wrinkled,
fierce, oblivious. Mary Ann studied her, looking as she always did
for some sign of herself in this little brown child with the fluffy hair.
A pint of white mixed with a gallon of black. She had been blended
in. But maybe it was always like this, children could not mirror or
repeat you. They went their own way.

Mary Ann's mother: Go on, heap dirt on our heads. I'm telling
everyone who asks, you're adopted. Then when they see you running
off to live with the niggers, they'll think you have nigger in you yourself. That'll probably make you happy.

And her father saying Now that's enough, over and over again.
Embarrassed eyes that would not meet hers. And she hated him
almost as much because he was weak, he would never stand up for
her.

So much taken from her. Like the struggle to wake in the white,
white room, swimming to the surface of consciousness and pain,
then learning she had lost seven whole weeks. Even now, sometimes
she woke gasping and numb. *How long had she slept?*

So much taken from her. She saw things flatly, like a child's
drawing with everything lined up on the horizon. She learned to

make her voice light and careless when she had to, never admitting loss, not letting anything else be taken. Humming, she looked out the window.

Wide pale sky and hills like a rumpled bedsheet. Khaki-colored grass and outcroppings of red rock. An arid, silent landscape whose foreignness excited them. On the horizon, a dark line which they hoped was mountains. The new eight-track stereo cartridge tape sang:

> He-ey, tonight
> Gonna be the night
> Gonna fly right to the sky
> Tonight

then

> He-ey, *chunk*night
> Gonna *chunk* the night
> Gonna *rechunkrechunkre*
> *Chunkchunk*

Oh shit. The exhaust? Carburetor? Fuel pump? The truck spat and died as Bert eased it to the side of the road. Je-sus, said Bert, and flipped the music off. They waited, Bert until he controlled his anger, Mary Ann until he would tell her what was wrong. Without the singing and the comfortable noise of their motion, the huge hot sky seemed to press down on them. Bert got out and raised the hood. Restarted the engine, but it died in a fit of noise and stinging smoke. Dawn woke up and began to cry.

Great, said Bert. Just great. He thought of the Interstate, the smooth ordered road they could have taken if only she hadn't talked him out of it. Can't you get her quiet, he said. I got to think.

Oh sure, said Mary Ann. I'll just explain that to her.

Bert studied the map. I think we're about nine miles from Crowheart, he said over the screaming.

Neither the distance nor the name seemed to offer much hope. They looked out at the dry hills and empty road. We'll wait awhile, said Bert, and if nobody comes I'll start walking.

Walk? You're kidding, that'll take hours. Wait til somebody comes along.

Yeah, you want to spend the night here? Fifteen minutes, that's all I'll give it. He put as much decisiveness as he could into the statement, trying to forget the money he could feel ticking away even as he spoke.

Waiting. And waiting. Mary Ann rocked the baby into quiet; Dawn regarded them both with wide uncertain eyes. Just as Bert was about to look at his watch for the last time, the road behind them produced first noise, then a red glittering pickup with an over-the-cab camper. Well hallelujah, said Bert. He got out to stand on the shoulder with his arm raised. The truck approached, slowed, as if to get a good look at them—they could see a woman's face pressed to the glass, two kids in the back reading comics—then accelerated past.

The sun seemed ready to puncture the metal roof. Maybe they'll at least tell a garage we're out here, said Mary Ann when Bert got back in the truck and slammed the door.

Sure. If there is a garage. And if they have to stop for soda pop anyway. Assholes.

I still say let's wait.

Don't tell me what to do. I got enough problems already.

Well it's my problem too and I've got a say in it.

Well, you're the one who said to take this stupid road, he said, giving in to his impatience. I had enough of your good ideas.

Oh, so it's my fault? Who's the big-shot mechanic who said he could fix anything?

I don't have to listen to this, said Bert, getting out.

Bullshitter, she screamed, as he started down the highway. Go ahead. I won't be here when you get back.

But just then the road came to life again. A slow-moving '63 Chevy, blue-green and battered, rolled toward them, pulled ahead of the truck and stopped. Mary Ann watched Bert run back, lean over the driver's side. Both doors opened and two men, boys really, got out. Oh Christ, said Mary Ann. Indians.

One, the driver, had a barrel chest and squat legs, a sly wide face.

His hair was drawn into two braids which grazed his shoulders. The other was thinner, his black hair cut short and ruffled by the wind. Both of them wore jeans and stretched-out T-shirts. She guessed them to be about eighteen. They walked towards the truck and one, the thin one, glanced at her, an indifferent narrow-eyed look.

After a moment Bert opened the door. Come on, they'll give us a ride.

I'm not going anywhere with you. She was crying by now.

Man, he said, you are too much. You know where we are? On an Indian reservation. If you're waiting for the Boy Scouts you gonna wait awhile. Let's go.

No, she cried, and he raised his hand but did not hit her, not yet. Let's go, he repeated, dead-calm, and she opened the door, hating him.

The two boys slit their eyes at her but did not speak as she got in the back of the Chevy. Then the fat one said something to the other, words she did not understand. They're talking Indian, she thought faintly. Bert stared straight ahead.

Fifteen minutes of silent driving, and the Chevy pulled up to a whitewashed building set in a yard of tamped dirt. There were two gas pumps in front. Why are we stopping here, Bert and Mary Ann each wondered. Then they knew: this was Crowheart. Post Office, general store, gas, the works. When the car stopped Mary Ann got out and marched toward the building without speaking.

There was a porch of uneven boards shaded by the roof. On it several Indians, older men in work shirts and cowboy hats, were sitting. She approached and they stopped talking. There were no chairs left so she went to the end of the porch and leaned against the wall.

Bert came around the corner. We're going back to take a look at it, he said. Here's money for a drink or something. She would not answer or take the five-collar bill he extended, so he tucked it in her purse and walked away. She watched him get back in the Chevy and drive off into the brown hills.

The men, four or five of them, sat with their hands on their knees, as unmoving as lizards in the heat. The one nearest her stood up. Here Missy, he said, pointing. Here. His skin was sunblackened, his eyes held in nets of wrinkles. Thank you, she said. He nodded and walked inside.

Now she was seated among them. They did not look at her, and she realized this was a form of courtesy. She could sit here all day minding her own business. They would not disturb her. She was grateful for their indifference. There were worse things than that. She permitted herself a moment of thought for the stalled truck.

An hour later her eyes caught a pillar of shimmering dust on the road. The heat made it seem impossibly far away and slow. But at last the Chevy appeared, followed by the truck. Mary Ann stood up. Good-bye, she said. They ducked their heads in a kind of chorus, and she walked to the truck.

Bert opened the door for her but neither of them spoke.

In silence they watched the hills rise into dark pine-covered peaks, noted the looping track of the river beneath them.

Easier to travel a thousand miles and camp among strange tribes than it is to apologize.

Until Bert stopped the truck to gaze at the incredible range of ice-covered stone that lay before them. The green-floored valley and blue lake. The air had grown cool, scented with pine and sage.

Ready to quit fightin, Bert asked, looking through the windshield.

Yeah. Pride made her want to sound sullen, but when she opened her mouth her lungs filled with thin cold air, a giddy perfume that lifted her voice.

Hey, she asked him later, as they watched the afternoon sun slide down the peaks. What was wrong with the truck?

Loose condenser.

Did you have to pay them much?

Nothing. Bert grinned. I gave em some reefer. We had a little peace-pipe session.

Back on the interstate in Idaho. Anxious now, impatient to get there. Turning up their noses at the lava plains and ragged crests: they were going somewhere better. Driving without stopping, Bert and Mary Ann trading shifts.

They raced against hunger, stuffing their bellies with pasty hamburgers and chocolate. They'd figured two weeks, that's how long they could last until Bert found a job.

Ten stiff $20 bills in the lining of Mary Ann's purse.

2 weeks = 14 days.

(x) motel rooms @ $12 = ?

Gas. Groceries. Rent deposit? Even if he found a job, how long would it be until he got a paycheck?

Bert's eyes glazed at the sun-slick road, and he fought to make the numbers balance. How much had they spent? Where had it leaked away from them? You're tired, he told himself. Everything seems worse when you're tired. Try to sleep. He closed his eyes. Something heavy was burrowing its way into his dreams. Metal grating on metal. He opened his eyes to darkness, and a new grinding sound from the engine: *Rak. Rak. Rak.* Steadily increasing in tempo and authority.

It just started, said Mary Ann.

Take the next exit, Bert told her. There was nothing else to say. Each knew what the other was thinking.

In the fluorescent, hard-edged glare of the Shell station, the teen-aged gas jockey shook his head. Might be your points burned out. A cylinder not firing. Or the spark plug wires. We won't have a mechanic in here til seven ayem. In the Pine-Sol–stinking rest-room Bert splashed water on his face. He walked back to the truck, started it, listened to the idle for a moment, and pulled onto the highway.

We got to, he said, before Mary Ann could open her mouth. Even if the mechanic was here we couldn't pay him. Unless we decide to settle down right here. We'll just drive the damn thing into the ground and see how far it gets.

We're a hundred twenty miles from the border, said Mary Ann after a moment. When he looked again both she and the baby were asleep.

Drifting lights in the darkness. The shallow cone of highway illuminated before him. He would find a job. They would live out in the country and when they'd saved enough they would buy horses. Dully he repeated this until it diminished into sing-song. Every muscle in his body felt bulky and unyielding.

Why should he be doubting now? So what if the worst happened, the truck failed and they had to hustle for money. Couldn't they do that? He supposed they could, but his weariness went further. He longed to shrink the world into something finite, physical, easily confronted. He supposed he'd felt it was that way once, although it was hard to remember now, while he strained to stay awake in the humming darkness. Oh yeah, he could lick anything with one hand tied behind him. Blindfolded. On his knees. Whistling Dixie.

The engine settled into a steady chattering. It might quit at ten miles or at a thousand. The headlights caught a highway sign but it was some moments before its meaning penetrated. Oregon. They were in Oregon though they still had three hundred miles to go. Indifferently he swung his head from one gray window to another. Even when the flat red sun popped up like the No Sale tag of a cash register, revealing shallow wheat fields that might have been in Kansas, even then he felt no special despair or disappointment. Just cold fatigue and inattention.

Mary Ann felt Dawn's fingers rooting in her hair, then the new hot day on her face. The baby began to cry and she spoke to her without opening her eyes. But the cramp in her back, the steady jogging—*Where was she?* Gasping, she reached out for the baby, then blinked and looked around her.

Just as she never spoke of the pinched pain behind her glass eye, or the ragged bones that never quite healed, so now she regarded the dust and flatness around her and did not acknowledge them.

I bet you want to sleep, huh, she said, rubbing Bert's neck with one hand and maneuvering the baby toward her nipple with the other.

Pretty soon, he said, trying to match her calmness.

Got to stop and change her anyway, said Mary Ann. I think she had a busy night.

Yeah well, began Bert, but he stopped at a new noise from somewhere in the oily complications of the engine. Before he'd heard it a second time he had identified it. Backfiring. Thick blue smoke uncoiled from the tailpipe, obscuring the road behind them. Twelve miles to an exit, said Bert as the wheel jumped under his hand. Come on, give us a break.

The explosions were so loud that cars following them hung back, gathering courage to pass. Five more miles they wrung from the tortured engine. In the side mirror Bert noticed a white shape traveling in their wake, just visible through the fumes. Then it pulled alongside and stayed there.

He ignored it as long as he could, even though the trooper was motioning to him. Then the red dome light went on.

The bastard wants me to pull over, cried Bert. Don't he know I'll never get it started again? He wrenched the truck to the shoulder and tried to let it idle, but it stalled. They waited until the trooper came up to them.

Morning, he said, and they could tell from his face, how it pulled away once he saw them, like he had stepped in shit, what he was thinking. They'd seen that look before.

Having trouble? he asked. The trooper was a thin young black-haired man, with a peculiar smooth look to his face, as if the bones had stunted, and light restless eyes.

Yeah, said Bert, and opened the door so the trooper had to take a step back. Yeah, we got trouble.

Could I see your license please? Take it out of the plastic. His voice was colorless, not matching the politeness of his words.

Bert stood silently, knowing this was not the time to protest, not yet. The trooper studied the license, shifting from one foot to the other, then asked for the registration. When Mary Ann had produced it from the glove compartment, he asked Now where are you folks going?

Portland, said Bert.

Mind if I take a look in the back, said the man, not making it a question, as he loosened one of the ropes and angled his thin back so he could peer beneath the canvas. Bert followed him, standing close enough that the trooper felt his presence and squared his shoulders as he stood up.

Well now, he said, his light eyes looking just beyond Bert, his voice still neutral, you folks aren't going to be able to get any farther. You're violating the emission control standards.

We're going to the next exit. We'll get it fixed there.

The trooper shook his head and the flat shadow of his hat brim

crept over his flat face. Can't let you back on the highway. You
could cause an accident, all that smoke. You'll have to get it towed.
We can't afford a tow.

Well . . . he paused, and Bert could see how little effort he was
putting into his words; they were a script he was following, certain of
the outcome. The only other thing we can do is impound the vehicle.

No, said Bert, and in speaking he committed himself to doing
what was necessary. His very exhaustion was a strength now,
because it loosened his fury. He felt the hard crust of sweat on his
muscles, the syncopated popping of nerves, the white sunlight
twitching in his eyes, and knew he could unleash himself. He could
murder, in broad daylight with his bare hands. Then take his wife
and child some place far away, some place he could also fight for
them. No, he repeated, I think it would be better if we just went to
the next exit. And he waited, calmly, for what would happen now.

Later he would wonder how he had looked to the trooper. Something, the glazed blood in his eyes, the stance of his legs, had com-
municated craziness, danger. The trooper squinted and turned his
smooth neutral face from side to side like a puzzled bird. After a
moment Bert realized he was calculating the cost of retreat, how
much pride was involved.

Well, said the trooper, if you drive on the shoulder, slow, I mean
slow, with your flashers going, I guess you could make it.

Sure. Bert waited a few seconds, in case the trooper insisted on
some further instruction as a sop to his authority. But the man only
said OK then, his eyes still wandering, and walked to his car.

Bert waited until he was gone, then tried the engine. It started
noisily but seemed more willing than before. When they reached a
gas station Bert coaxed the mechanic into lending him tools,
changed the burnt-out points himself, handed the keys to Mary
Ann, and only then allowed himself sleep.

He woke, after how long he did not know, when Mary Ann cried
out. Smatter, he said, lurching upright. What? What?

But she was turning her head from side to side, trying to make her
one good eye take in all that was before her. The road was pulling
them toward a river, pulling them down then lifting to follow the

banks. A mile-wide stretch of misty water curving between raw brown cliffs. In the distance the road, and everything on it, dwindled to a thread. She strained her neck to see the top of the cliffs but it was all too large, it would not order itself into a single view.

Rounding a turn, she squinted. Floating above the horizon was a mass of slate and white, like a smeared cloud. Only it was no cloud. Bert saw it too, and they both opened their mouths to speak: Damn, that thing must be eighty miles away, look at it, just look. But the wind, which had increased steadily as they entered the gorge, now slammed against the truck and filled the air with its roaring. Mary Ann gripped the wheel tighter and turned to Bert. Their lips still worked, forming speech. It would take all their strength to make themselves heard.